To
Alex

What a Load of Rubbish

The story of a man's battle against mechanisation

(A story for children and childish adults)

Martin R. Etheridge

With love

Clink
Street

London | New York

Martin

xxx

Published by Clink Street Publishing 2015

Copyright © 2015

First edition.

ISBN: 978-1-910782-18-7
E-book: 978-1-910782-19-4

I have a lot of people to thank for my recovery. First and foremost my Aunt Vi - we "shared" many a meal together at Q.E.M.H. Woolwich when I was a patient in the "Cabbage Patch".

Secondly my Mum, Eileen (sadly no longer with us but always with me); my Dad, Norman (down to earth and salt of the earth); my Uncle, Harold (everyone should have one) and my brother, Kev (although we fight like cat and dog we always have a laugh).

Thirdly, my son, Jack "the flatfoot" - sorry, Policeman and my daughter, Rosie C, now a mum herself. Lastly, to "Brazillian bombshell" Teressa Mendonça, my best friend ever, love always,

Martin
XXXXXX

Table of Contents

BEFORE WE BEGIN

If you have opened this book expecting to find a tale of witches and wizards flying around on broomsticks then I'm sorry, you are going to be disappointed – there is no sorcery in this book. The only brooms mentioned are used in the way they were intended to be, that is to sweep up rubbish. There is magic though, real magic, but that comes later – like all good things.

Chapter 1
The Wonderful 'All-In-One-Der'

Suburbiaville Council works depot yard looked as though a bomb had struck. There were sheets of paper of all sizes and colours, paper bags, cardboard boxes, carrier bags, polythene bags with who knows what insid1e. There were broken bottles and smashed crockery from the works depot kitchen, week old left-overs from staff breakfasts. These were mixed in with used industrial tea-bags – the big ones from the four-gallon urns, and mountains of coffee dregs. The big, outside ashtrays had been upturned and emptied all over the concrete, along with all the sand from the fire buckets.

The office staff had emptied their waste-paper baskets, the cleaning staff had thrown the contents of a number of vacuum cleaner bags out on the ground. A chilly wind blew in through the gates stirring all this into a thick, cold, inedible stew. Sheets of bubble-wrap and wads of tissue packaging had been slung willy-nilly all over the area – on top of this mechanics from the Motor Transport Wing had dumped all the greasy rags, engine and sump oil, old brake and clutch fluid. The yard was an unsightly oily slick, dotted here and there with debris – the top of a cake sprinkled with hundreds and thousands. And it smelled. It smelled of… of, uurrgh, words cannot describe the smell.

"Okay, Geordie," called Willie Eckerslike across the council works depot yard, "power 'er up, lad. I said. Power 'er up!"

"Reet y'are, Mr Eckerslike, like." Just outside the gates a tatty head, the hair scraggy and thinning under a cloth cap, ducked below the dashboard of a truck, the engine whirred a couple of times – a powerful beast gunned into life – and settled down to a deep purr.

"Bring 'er in lad. I said. Bring 'er in!" Willy shouted above the rumble, hardly able to contain himself. A few revs, a gear-change and the huge beast crawled through the double-gates and into the yard. Air-brakes released. Hissed like a hundred angry pythons, the throttle opened wide and the vehicle lurched forward coming to a halt inside the double-gates. A grinding wrench from the hand brake, a door opened and Geordie jumped down from the drivers' cab, rubbing his hands together.

Mister Willy Eckerslike hopped from foot to foot like a startled pigeon, hardly able to control his excitement – the other pigeons just coo-cooed and flew away. It was such a thrill to watch his plan start to take shape. Mister Willy Eckerslike was the rather round Managing Director of Suburbiaville Newtown Council. A blunt, brash, self-made man from "Up-North" with a bald pate and double-chin – who had his beady eye on the Mayoral Elections, taking place next year. He had "come from nowt" and "grafted f' perishin' years to get where 'e is today". Where he was, now, was at the end of a very large "Winston Churchill" cigar that looked very impressive but he never lit it: "I'm not payin' out good money on cigars to watch 'em go up in smoke," he used to say, or rather shout, "I said. I'm not payin' out good money on cigars to set fire to 'em!" Besides Missus Eckerslike would not tolerate the smell of them in the house. And Willy was master in his own home – wasn't he?

Mister Eckerslike was an ex-school bully. He had passed all his exams at school, but on the very last day of term had managed to get himself expelled for thumping a Physical Training teacher. The story goes that this poor teacher was fresh out of training college, and had tried to make the young Willy do press-ups during the lesson but he wasn't "Grovellin' on t'floor for no beggar." He wasn't reluctant to throw his weight around, was our Willy. His whole philosophy on life was, "Y'can't mek an omelette wi'out breakin' a few 'eads."

"Here y'are Mister Eckerslike, like. All the way from 'Umberside mon," sang Geordie in a high-pitched, Tyneside warble. "One brand new, state-of-the-art, fully automat'd, self-supportin', boil-in-the-bag, 'All-in-One-Der'." Geordie wasn't the sharpest tack in the box but could read his operating manual well enough to learn it by heart. And add a couple of his own embellishments: "Complete with self-emptyin', rechargeable Rubbish Robots – DA-daaaah!"

Willy Eckerslike flushed proudly at his new toy, then, "Well, go on, lad," his big, flabby cheeks glowing redder and redder. "I said go on –" getting more and more excited, "Let's see what she can do!" bullying Geordie back into the cab. "… And where's that beggar Bartholemew – 'e better be 'ere or I'll 'ave his job, I said. I'll 'ave 'is job, So 'elp me!"

"Oh – er – um – I'm here Mister Eckerslike, sir, god and infinitely more important person than myself." Gordon

4

Bartholemew ran out of the works depot building straightening his tie, brushing the dust from his suit which was a little too big for him – it made him look a touch weedier than he actually was. He was explaining and excusing himself even before he had Mister Eckerslike's ear, not that Willy ever listened.

"Save it, Bartholemew, I didn't get where I am today by listening t' your perishin' excuses." Mister Eckerslike repeated just to make sure he was understood. "I said. I didn't get where I am today by listenin' t'worms like you…"

But Gordon Bartholemew was determined to get his point across. He nearly ran Willy over trying to get himself in place before his absence was noticed. He failed and attempted to redeem himself. "I've been here all the time, sir – so there really is no need to fire me, sir – but you were so *engrossed* in what you were doing – um – sir, god and infinitely mo…"

"Alright, Bartholemew, don't overdo it now. I said, don't overdo it!" But secretly Mr Eckerslike enjoyed being grovelled to; it swelled his already inflated ego. "I want thee to stand 'ere and watch me put this 'All-in-One-Der' through its paces. I said, I want you to…"

"Yes sir, god and inf…"

"Shuttit Bartholemew!"

"Yessir!"

"Reet – Geordie lad. Go on – show

Bartholemew 'ere what she can do.

"Okay Mister Eckerslike, like – watch oot noo..." And the "All-in-One-Der" changed up a gear and rumbled forward. Geordie had to shout very loudly so that his voice would reach Messrs. Eckerslike and Bartholemew and compete against the loud throbbing rumble coming from the engine.

"Can I draw yer attention, like," he yelled, "Tee the specially designed, rotatin' interchangeable, reinforced steel brushes under each o' the front wheels!"

"Speak up, I can't 'ear yer!" shouted Mister Eckerslike. "I said. I can't 'ear a piggin' word you're sayin', lad!" So Geordie stuck an arm out of the window and pointed down at the front wheel. "It's th' same on th' other side, look!" Clouds of dust rose on either side of the truck as brushes whirled beneath, pushing it to the front of the vehicle, scoring faint circles in the concrete.

"Noo th' rotatin' brush at th' front can sweep it all ahead t'be picked-up seconds later by the Rubbish Robots!" cried Geordie, driving the "All-in-One-Der" slowly forward, yelling above the engine noise, and pushing all the dust, dirt, pieces of paper, oily rags and other accumulated debris into a neat pile at the far end of the yard.

"B-But," Gordon Bartholemew stammered, pointing at the pile of rubbish that had built up.

"Shurrup, Bartholemew. I said, shur-rup, I'm demonstratin'." Willy Eckers-like silenced him with a hard stare and a frown, and a backhander in the ribs. "I'm demonstratin', I said. Go on, Geor-die lad," he hollered, "do y'perishin' stuff – I said. Do yer chuffin' stuff!"

"Reet y'are, Mister Eckerslike, like." This was the party-piece he'd been dying to show off ever since the factory had released the truck into his care. He announced proudly, "I will noo demon-strate the awesome speed and fully auto-matic agility of the Rubbish Robot! – of which there are four, like."

Messrs. Eckerslike and Bartholemew watched Geordie's head disappear below the dashboard in the cab as he bent down to flick the switches on the control-box to the "on" position.

A couple of clicks, followed by a whir-ring noise, and stabilisers appeared behind each wheel securing the beast to the ground.

The truck shuddered, let out a long mechanical yawn and cantilever doors opened vertically, between the hopper – which held the refuse – and the driv-er's cab. The big "All-in-One-Der" now appeared like a great flying insect, with wings outstretched, about to take flight. But it didn't move. Rather than soaring into the air, a small squad of fourwheelie

-bins on tracks rolled out, down a ramp and onto the ground, and took up position two on each side of the great wagon, like mechanical chicks nestling under their mother's wings – bleeping occasionally, humming quietly and constantly. These droids were each equipped with movable arms fitted with interchangeable tools, such as a broom, a scoop, a steam hose and a grab which operated like a person's hand.

The wheelie-bins lined up, two on either side of the vehicle, with all their attachments stored in shelves and recesses built into its body looking for all the world like soldiers kitted up and ready to go into battle. Again, Geordie ducked down to the control-box and flicked on another switch...

Invisible to the naked eye, inaudible to the untrained ear, an electrical message flashed from an antenna on the roof of the driver's cab to a micro-chip in the lid of each bin. This micro-chip was the wheelie-bin's "brain" and once alerted, each bin tore into the pile of rubbish that the "All-in-One-Der" had pushed up into a huge pile at the far end of the council works depot yard.

Cardboard boxes, small or large and even the huge ones, were broken down into smaller, more manageable pieces by the grab and fed into an oversized paper and card-shredder installed into the top of the lid of each wheelie-bin.

Oily rags, any wet paper, sand, paint – anything you like that had a sticky, damp or glutinous element to it – was sucked directly into the bins' gut by a "nifty" suction device situated underneath as the robotic bin drove over it. The robotic bin would then return seconds later to the oily patch, paint stain, or whatever it was and scrub it clean with rotating brushes fitted beneath the bins, between the tracks. The Rubbish Robots would then drive over the area again and again: ducking and diving, sucking and scrubbing – weaving intricate patterns and figures of eight over the stains on the ground, until they were there no longer.

Fitted dead in the centre of each robot bin was a bright red, flashing sensor that would seek out and identify any rubbish or anything that should not have been there – this was the bin's "eye". Then, using its Artificial Intelligence Chip, it would work out in fragments of a second how to deal with it. For example, whether to bin it, scrub it, shred it or suck it up and store it. Each time the bin filled itself up, it would make a cute little "burping" sound – like a baby being "winded" – and return to the "All-in-One-Der" in order to empty itself into the "Crusher".

The "Crusher" looked much the same as the device on many everyday garbage trucks, and it was – only it was twice as big, twice as powerful, and twice as fast.

Munching, scrunching, cracking, crunching, swallowing, digesting – it could deal with anything the little droid bins could throw at it, or in it, in hardly any time at all.

"This is wonderful," exclaimed Willy Eckerslike, "absolutely piggin' wonderful. I said it once and I'll say it twice, piggin' wonderful..."

"Er, actually sir, that's three times," cut in Mr. Bartholemew, eager to re-enter Willy's good books – he failed again.

"Shuttit, Bartholemew..."

"Yessir!"

Gordon Bartholemew did as he was told. Willy Eckerslike went on, "Aye – this will revolutionise street cleaning. I said, it'll revolutionise street cleaning. I'll save t'council so much money they'll be beggin', I said *beggin'* me t'become t'Mayor by this time next year, by 'eck, Bartholemew, an' I 'ope your takin' notes, I said. Are you takin' notes?"

"Er – yes, sir, I am," mumbled Gordon Bartholemew, quaking in his Hush Puppy, slip-on shoes, dropping his note book on the wet ground. "B-but won't that put a lot of people out of work?" adding thoughtfully, "Some have got families to feed, you know." "Perishin' 'eck Bartholemew, who needs mere humans..." Willy let out an exasperated gasp. "I said, who needs mere piggin' 'umans – when my 'Rubbish Robots' can do twice as much work in 'alf t'perishin' time. And…" He put the icing on the cake. "We don't 'ave to pay them, norra penny. I said norra brass razoo!"

"Th-th-then w-what will happen to me, sir!" Gordon moaned desolately.

"When I am t'chuffin' Mayor, I said, *when* I am t'Mayor. You…" Willy added gleefully, his tone became lighter, not so loud, "…will continue as my underling. I said you will carry on as my whipping boy! I need lirr'l people like you to mek me look big!"

"Thank you, sir!" grovelled Gordon Bartholemew, grateful to find out that he would still have a job. "Thank you…" This made him feel slightly bolder. "But sir, this machine will put people like Malcolm, a dedicated artist, out of work."

"*WHO?*"

But not very much bolder: "Nothing, sir, I'll speak to him…" But he never did. The trial came to an end. Job done. The Rubbish Robots lined up at bottom of the ramp, then, like hungry school-children in the dinner queue, hummed and bleeped their way up it into the "All-in-One-Der".

One last job: Geordie switched off the control box, and the cantilever doors closed automatically shutting the "Rubbish Robots" safely inside. Then he switched off the engine and locked up the vehicle until the following Monday morning.

Mister Bartholemew never did find Malcolm to tell him. If only he had issued Malcolm with a walkie-talkie then he'd have been able to call him in, but it was one of those things that he hadn't got round to doing. So he just forgot – an easy thing to do with a chap like Malcolm. He was so reliable.

Yes, that was it. He was just so reliable he didn't need one, and a bit thick too – he'd probably only break it.

****

Switched off, locked-up and left unmanned with the 'Rubbish Robots' stored inside, in its council colours of green and mustard-yellow, glistening with streaks of early morning rain, speckled with dirt from the trial, the "All-in-One-Der" looked like a large, fat toad that had crawled out of the river. With headlamps dimmed, its eyes were closed – it was asleep. Resting in silence, waiting patiently until those robots fed it on Monday morning, filling that ever hungry hopper – *the belly of the beast.*

Chapter 2

It's in My Blood

Early Monday morning on Willowy Lane, a long residential road in Suburbiaville, a new town on the Essex/North-East London border. There was the British Rail station with a snack-bar in the waiting room at one end of the lane, and the town park at the other. This meant that on a hot day, if you bought an ice-cream from the kiosk at the station, it would melt long before you could get to the park and enjoy it while sat on a bench, unless you had a cool-box. There was, too, a little hardware outlet that sold cool-boxes next to the station.

Suburbiaville Newtown was idyllic, the home of doctors, lawyers, court judges, stockbrokers and television celebrities.

Oh yes, and rumour has it that a Hollywood movie star used it as a holiday home. Only those who could afford to lived in Suburbiaville. Of course it had its less desirable areas, like most places, but the residents of Willowy Lane refused to recognise those areas as part of Suburbiaville. To live anywhere near Willowy Lane you needed to be very successful indeed and have a face that fitted – oh, and an air of snobbishness didn't go amiss.

Malcolm was a street cleaner from the other, *less* desirable, side of town. He cleaned Willowy Lane and the other streets nearby. He was hard working, dedicated and so clean and tidy it was untrue. Street cleaners who cleaned other, less desirable parts of Suburbiaville Newtown would turn up for work in a tatty old donkey jacket or jeans and stained shirt, creased and crumpled from the day before, but not Malcolm.

Malcolm wore a donkey jacket like the others but his always looked smart, clean and well looked after. And the "Suburbiaville Council Street Cleaning Services" logo on the "Hi-Way Vest" he wore was written in the same Day-Glo fiery-orange paint that coloured his barrow – smartness, visibility and safety was one of his mottoes. Every Friday after work he would call in at the dry cleaners just outside the town centre to have the jacket cleaned, pressed and any scuffs or tears invisibly mended. He got on very well with Mister Patel, a cockney from Bangladesh, who owned "Pat's Perfect Drycleaners" and because Malcolm would, sometimes, clean outside his shop front on his way home from work even though this wasn't part of his pitch, Mister Patel, sometimes, would not charge him any money for the cleaning or repair. And, sometimes, Malcolm would pay for cleaning and repairs – they had an easy going relationship.

Malcolm would turn up for work each day clean-shaven with just a hint of delicately fragranced aftershave, hair slicked back and teased into a smart coiff, sharply creased turned-up trousers, a tie and smart fashionably-cut shirt. Or in the summer, he would leave the tie on a rack with the others – a different one with a clean shirt for every day of the week – and opt for the open-necked look with turned up sleeves. As for the donkey jacket, it would be draped over the handle of his barrow giving an almost "couldn't-care-less" impression. But rest assured this was all a ruse; about his image Malcolm cared a great deal. And he would spend a good hour in the morning preparing himself for work.

Whether it was winter or summer Malcolm's shoes outshone the best boots of the smartest guardsman on the Queen's birthday parade and his belt buckle positively shone like spun gold whatever the weather.

Malcolm pushed a barrow like no other with racing tyres on the wheels, two galvanised steel dustbins, one in front of the other, and a compartment on one side for his brooms, and quick-release clips on the other for his trusty pooper-scooper. For Malcolm could never tell when his skill and dexterity may face the ultimate test. It might be that a pooch had "pooed" on the pavement or some yobbo had "gobbed" a thick, sticky wad of chewing-gum on the path. Malcolm knew from experience that, like with most everyday things, a pooper-scooper had more than just one use. It was fitted with an air-tight snap-and-seal lid, operated by a trigger-lever installed in the hand-grip. The long-handled device would seal off any odour or germs that may try to escape, thus preventing risk of infection or atmospheric contamination.

His barrow was equipped with wing-mirrors, giving him a good field of vision to the rear because as cars were being designed to run more and more quietly these days, he needed to be sure that he could pull into the side of the road at a moment's notice when sweeping roadside gutters and avoid motorists on those dark mornings. Headlamps that

ensured a good view ahead were pow-
ered by a rechargeable battery which
was kept "topped-up" by a nifty little
dynamo attachment he had designed,
made and fitted himself in a shed in his
backyard.

That shed was a shrine to his equipment. Hanging from the corrugated
ceiling were replacement cords for his
"helping hand", the tool he used to pick
up paper – lest one snapped. And, of
course, for the snap-and-seal device on
his pooperscooper. On the walls were
spare wheels because one could quite
easily be buckled during a frenzy of
urban enhancement, and tyres as Malcolm was always picking up punctures.
For example, when cleaning cross-coun-
try, pine needles embedded themselves
in a tyre and mending punctures was
one of those annoying little tasks that
had to be done regularly if one wanted
to be as efficient as Malcolm.

In the corner of his shed was a block-
and-tackle, which Malcolm would rig
up each year as summer drew to a close,
in order to hoist his barrow to the ceiling and re-spray it a fiery orange colour
in Day-Glo paint. Being seen, Malcolm
maintained, is as much a part of safety
as being able to see – this was another of
Malcolm's mottos, of which he had many.
And stacked in an opposite corner were
bottles of disinfectant which he would

use every day after work, often labouring well into the evening if his equipment was particularly dirty.

Yes, Malcolm loved his barrow and he was prepared to put in hours of unpaid overtime making sure it was clean, tires pumped-up and ready to go at all times – this labour of love was the reason he, sometimes, worked well into the night. It, or "she" if Malcolm was in earshot, even had a name: "Belinda", or "Bel" for short but only he could call her that.

And what's more, if it is possible, the barrow seemed to love him. There seemed to be an uncanny connection between man and machine. It understood every little change in the pressure of his hands as Malcolm pushed.

Suburbiaville Central British Rail station sat on top of the hill at the end of Willowy Lane – a very steep, one-in-four gradient; now remember this, it could turn out to be important. Part of Malcolm's job was to clean up one side of the lane in time to be able to nip in and sweep up after all the commuters had gone to their work in London, Birmingham or farther away. And they were a messy lot – always leaving newspapers, plastic cups and other intercity travellers' debris lying all over the place.

As Malcolm would push up the gradient towards Suburbiaville Central, the wheels would free themselves, taking full advantage of the expensive lubricant that he bought himself and lavished on the axles. Then, on the way back down the hill "Belinda" would apply a friction of her own, so that rather than rolling away out of Malcolm's control he would have to push it ever so gently down the hill, thus allowing him to flow smoothly onto the other side of the lane. Now if that isn't an example of a man's perfect relationship with his machine, what is?

Of course, there is always that chance of a break-down in this relationship, as many racing-car drivers or cyclists are aware, a glob of oil too many or insufficient tyre pressure. So far that had not happened. But just in case it did, Malcolm had another "nifty" little device incorporating an anchor and a "deadman's handle", which he'd won playing cards with an underground train driver.

This, fingers crossed, had never happened either but, just in case it did, Malcolm kept it clean, well lubricated and tested it every evening. You could never be sure, could you?

You might think that all these attachments and safety additions would make this barrow quite cumbersome and pretty hard to push. And you would be quite correct. But Malcolm was an artist who used his skill and knowledge of oils and lubricants to keep his barrow rolling smoothly at all times. And the extra weight kept his shoulders and arms muscular, his wrists supple. Oh yes, quite a hunk was Malcolm.

You see, being a street cleaner was the only thing that Malcolm had ever wanted to be, even when he was small. *His* father and his father's father. His father and his father's father too; the Tilsleys had a long family history of street cleaning, who do you imagine had cleaned up the beaches after the allied evacuation at Dunkirk?

And before that during the English Civil War do you think anyone, other than a Tilsley, would have risked life and limb tidying up after those cavaliers and roundheads had churned-up Turnham Green with their horses' hooves? And somebody had to sweep up all those musket balls – that had been a Tilsley.

Remember the Norman Invasion, when King Harold got an arrow in the eye? No, maybe you had not been born yet – but you can bet your pocket money that a Tilsley had been there too. Clearing away all those bows and arrows so that the ambulance men could come, stretcher King Harold off the field and patch up his eye in safety.

Going back even farther in time, long before town councils were ever invented, even before there was a Suburbiaville, probably, there was many a caveman who was grateful to a Tilsley, for sweeping piles of dinosaur droppings from the front of his cave.

Rumour had it – "Well, it's more than a rumour really," mentioned his father once, "That it was a Tilsley who piled up those stones so neatly at Stonehenge."

Malcolm listened to stories such as these at his father's knee, so you can imagine the dismay of the careers master when he asked: "And what would you like to be when you leave school, young man?"

And Malcolm answered, "I want to be a professional street cleaner…"

It was as though Malcolm had got up and punched him on the nose. "What did you say, young Tilsley, a *street cleaner*?" Perhaps the man hadn't heard correctly – oh, but he heard alright, much to his dismay, when Malcolm repeated, "I want to be a professional street cleaner."

"But your exam marks are splendid – people would commit *murder* to obtain marks like yours," the careers master exclaimed. "Of all things, why do you want to be a street cleaner?"

You see, Malcolm wasn't thick; he was just down to earth and wasn't afraid of manual labour – the thought of carrying on his family's tradition swelled his chest with pride. But if he was going to carry the family torch, then it would shine brighter than it ever had in previous years.

The careers master was becoming

quite emotional – and he was beginning to stammer. "Y-You could b-be anything you wanted to be – a lawyer. How about oceanic acquisition – think of all that oil? Think of all that *money*? Why do you want to be a street cleaner of all things?"

"Sir," answered Malcolm very seriously, "you don't understand, I want to be a *professional* street cleaner – the best street cleaner there ever was, the best there ever will be."

The careers master tried to put him off this crazy idea; he could not understand this lack of ambition. "B-but street cleaners are ten-a-penny – nobody *wants* to be a street cleaner. Uurrgh! Think of all that dog mess. *Please* be sensible, don't waste your talents, young man."

"Waste my talents?" replied Malcolm. "Waste my talents? It's in my blood – my father was a street cleaner." He went on, "And so was 'is father and 'is father and 'is father's father – oh yeah, and his father and his father before him… Oh yeah and –" Malcolm related his family history, describing in detail the *vital* part played by the Tilsley family in the Wars of the Roses and the Dunkirk evacuation.

The careers master was quite shaken. "Have you ever considered a career in medi…" But he never quite got to the end of the sentence. Malcolm cut him off dead.

"And why do you think those stones are

piled up so neatly at Stone'enge?" reasoned Malcolm to the careers master.

This was too much. The poor careers master started to tear his hair.

"That's quite enough, young Tilsley, I wash my hands of you and when I've washed them, I'll make a phone call." He rubbed his hands together theatrically and made the call and the following Monday, Malcolm was interviewed by a rather thin, quite nervous Mister Bartholemew, who sent him upstairs to Mister Eckerslike who glowered at him and muttered grudgingly.

"Alreet – y'young beggar, but I 'ope you like you like 'ard graft. I said I 'ope you like 'ard work or I'll fire you before t'week is out!" Then he sent Malcolm back downstairs to Mister Bartholemew who issued him with slightly oversized overalls, a donkey jacket and orders to, "Report here at 8-30 sharp, next Monday morning!"

At 8-15 the following Monday morning Malcolm stood outside Suburbiaville Council works depot yard, fresh-faced and clean-shaven. His donkey jacket had been tailored, courtesy of a Mister Patel, proprietor of a newly opened "Pat's Perfect Dry Cleaners". It fit like a glove and he was wearing a clean shirt and a tie.

Mister Bartholemew was most impressed by this new lad's punctuality and turn-out. "Good morning, young man!" he smiled, doffing his hat and wondering how long this enthusiasm would last.

Five minutes later Mister Eckerslike turned up in his BMW and grunted, "Oh it's thee – go an' see Bartholemew an'e will issue thee wi' a barrow. Well, go on, I said. Go an' see my underling an' he will gi'yer your new barrow."

On that very morning Malcolm was issued with a barrow. Okay, so it was pretty battered and a bit rickety, having seen better days but over the years Malcolm kept adding *little improvements* until it came to look as it does today – large, bulky, bright orange, shiny and unwieldy with mirrors and headlights. You see, Malcolm took his occupation very seriously indeed. He did not simply clean streets. He *purged* public thoroughfares.

Over the years, news of Malcolm's sterling work reached the ears of HRH the Queen herself, and he was summoned to a royal garden party to receive an award for public service "above and beyond the call of duty". Unfortunately, he was unable to attend, so he wrote a letter, "respectfully declining" her "most kind and generous invitation" saying that as the garden party took place on a Monday he had to be on duty, to clean up Willowy Lane and the surrounding area. Therefore, would "Her Majesty mind terribly if he did not attend and received the honour by post instead". He signed it, "Your most loyal public servant, Malcolm Tilsley". As Her Majesty had no idea where to put Malcolm's unwieldy barrow during the ceremony in the royal stables, not without upsetting the horses *and* the corgis, she was only too pleased with his idea and quickly wrote back agreeing.

****

After that interview, Malcolm's careers master was never the same. Never in his long career had he met a pupil with ambitions of becoming a street cleaner – the poor man just could not get his head round it. What child *wants* to sweep roads for a living? Some weeks later, he booked himself into a home for "tired and retired intellectuals", where he is still a resident to this day *twenty-seven years later*. He sits alone in his room, still tearing at what little hair he has left; still trying to fathom the reason – WHY?

Chapter 3

Malcolm and the Power of the Pooperscooper

Early morning on the very swish, slightly snooty Willowy Lane, birds sang in the acacia trees, a milk-float drove along stopping every few houses so that the milkman could take away the empties and put fresh pints on the doorsteps, whistling cheerfully as he did so. Children went to school, a gentle breeze blew down the street rustling the leaves in the trees and the faint "dah-daah" sounded from an express-train as it hurtled through Suburbiaville Central station.

Malcolm had been *on parade* since eight-thirty that morning making sure people could travel to work in safety, without slipping on any oily or greasy patches, banana skins or, God forbid, some pooch had "pooed" on the pavement. So far, ever since Malcolm had started working the Willowy Lane patch, this hadn't happened but just in case it did, he was there, no more than an arm's stretch away from his trusty broom and pooperscooper.

So it happened that on one day in particular, this is exactly what did. Malcolm was sizing up his day's work, calculating the wind direction. Flexing his muscles, shifting his weight from foot to foot and mentally preparing himself to embark on a frenzy of urban enhancement. When on the far side of the street, he spotted the potential hazard. At a distance of about eighty metres away his eagle eye picked out an enormous dollop of doggy-doo. On his patch this was unthinkable – his whole reputation was at risk. The canine offender, probably a stray from a less desirable area, had only just fled the scene of the crime and had Malcolm looked, he would have just spotted its furry tail disappearing around a corner. An evil smelling vapour was escaping from the nauseous mound, a sort of testament to its freshness.

Then disaster loomed. Malcolm heard a door open, loud smacking noises when kisses were blown, with a cheery, "Goodbye darling!" Followed by a *CRASH!* as the door slammed shut. A smartly dressed city gent stepped out of his front garden on the same side of the street. He wore a pin-striped suit, collar and tie, and cuff-links. The whole ensemble was completed by the shiniest and most expensive looking pair of shoes that Malcolm had ever seen, with a silver bar across each instep. The man was reading a paper – the stocks and shares page. So engrossed was he in the facts and figures before his eyes that he failed to spot the dollop of disease lying directly in his path. Neither did he see the noxious vapours escaping, threatening to contaminate everything within a five metre radius.

Clip-clop, clip-clop; the city gent and this remarkably shiny, remarkably expensive pair of shoes were *en route* for disaster. And judging by that slight squeaking noise they were probably brand new.

Malcolm realised he had only seconds in which to act. The *Theme from Jaws* played over and over in his imagination. But he did not panic. In an amazing feat of mental agility he worked out the approximate distance from himself to the city gent. Then, in a split-second, he gauged the distance between man and mess and carefully divided this by the estimated cost of the shoes, and added the time it would take him to whip out his broom and pooperscooper from his barrow, plus or minus three seconds for wind resistance. If this isn't more than adequate use of my scientific and mathematical skills, thought Malcolm, I don't know what is.

He snatched his equipment from the barrow and set out at a flat run – covering the distance across the street with only a flea's breath to spare.

He reached the man just as he was about to plunge his foot into the odorous ooze, then, performing a dainty half-pirouette that would have left many a professional ballet dancer speechless. An action which prevented the gent from transferring his weight onto

his forward foot – an act which would have carried the man *GLITCH* into the putrid poo. Then our Malcolm slid the pooperscooper into position and with a slide and a gentle flick of his broom, *scooped the poop* into the *scoop* and depressed the trigger-lever on the snap-and-seal device. And the malicious matter was encased in an air-tight compartment, which prevented any escape of fumes into the atmosphere. The movement was completed when Malcolm spun on his heel, and bent low at the waist to spray a little water over the affected area, straightening a millisecond later to provide a human cushion for the gent to bump into. The whole incident was over in less than a heartbeat.

The gent, until the moment he walked

into Malcolm's braced shoulders, crumpling his newspaper and knocking his spectacles forward on his nose, was completely unaware of all this activity going on about him – he didn't even realise Malcolm was there...

"Ooff, oh – ahh – ouch!" An instance of annoyance. "What the Devil..?" The gent glared angrily at Malcolm. Then he looked down at the fading stain on the pavement, looked up and saw Malcolm standing over it – a slight sheen of perspiration on his brow.

The gent's face broke into a smile as he pieced together what had happened. "Why thank you, very much – I could have stepped straight into that, would've ruined my shoes, do you know how much I paid for these?" he gasped, flexing an outstretched foot, looking down at his at his gleaming footwear.

"Why, that's alright, sir," Malcolm returned, "You could've 'ad a nasty accident there sir – oh aye," he continued in his Essex drawl, "I've seen it afore, a lady, two enormous bags o' shoppin' – she didn't see..." Shaking his head he went on to explain, "A banana – half-eaten on the pavement. She slipped – shoppin' all over the place. I visit 'er in 'ospital from time to time, sir. A shadder of 'er former self, sir. A mere shadder – 'asn't been the same since..."

"But do you realise how much money

you saved me?" The city gent thrust a hand into his back pocket, brought out a bulging wallet and fished out a five pound note. "You really must allow me to reward you..."

"No – no – no sir. Put yer money away – or else I'll be offended."

"Then how?" A frown crinkled on the city gent's brow.

"Sir!" Malcolm squared his jaw and put on a most determined expression. "Just knowin' that you're safe and well is reward enough fer me. I was born to this – it's my mission in life. It's in my blood, Tilsley's the name, Malcolm Tilsley. Did you know there has been a Tilsley cleanin' up after every significant event in British 'istory?" He held out the palms of his hands, in an "it's as simple as that" gesture and said, "Those stones at Stonehenge didn't pile themselves up, you know..."

Then he went on to describe in detail the role of his ancestors in a variety of military campaigns through the ages, starting with the allied evacuation at Dunkirk. Going back further to describe the battle of Agincourt and, don't forget, The Wars of the Roses.

"Of course, Shakespeare doesn't mention a Tilsley in any of 'is books, sir – us people who do the dirty work are soon forgotten." Adding, "But we're the *real* 'eroes – who d'ya think cleared them bows an' arrows off the beaches at the battle of 'Astings so that the paramedics could stretcher King 'Arold off the field. *That* had been a Tilsley, sir... Sir?"

"*SNORE...*"

Malcolm's family history had been a little too long and drawn-out to hold the gent's attention for very long; his mind began to wander. As Malcolm rattled episode after episode of his family history off by heart, the gent had sat on a garden wall and drifted off to sleep. He was woken by Malcolm shaking him gently by the shoulder, with a start he came to life. "Oh – er – *YAWN*! Sorry Malcolm, you were saying..."

But Malcolm didn't mind. "No – no – no, sir – I goes on a bit sometimes." There was an awkward silence, then:

"Yes – well, thank you again, Malcolm. Now I must catch my train – time is money you know." And he was off – in the direction of Suburbiaville British Rail station, leaving Malcolm to replace his pooperscooper and broom on his barrow for the next time. This was not the first time something like this had happened – and Malcolm very much doubted it would be the last.

"Look mum, there's Malcolm!" a small child's voice called down the street. The sound reached Malcolm's ears just as he was putting away his brooms and pooperscooper, his eyes scanning from one side of the street to the other, searching for any rubbish he may have missed.

"Can we go and see him, mum? Can we, can we?"

"Oh alright Jack," the young mum sighed and gave in. "But hold your sis..." But it was too late. The small boy galloped off down the street in the direction of Malcolm then came to a screeching halt when his mother's voice rang out. "Jack, wait for your sister. Rosie – hold Jack's hand!" A hint of rising panic in the lady's voice.

"Now, now, now – don't you worry, missus!" Malcolm's practised country drawl would assure the young mum; the woman would never guess at his level of education. To her, Malcolm was just another manual worker, one of the lesser educated types who cleaned the streets – no particular ambition in life. All the same, he was an extremely nice chap, and so good to the children – her pride and joy.

"I've got my eye on 'em! And 'ave they been bin good children for their mum?"

"Oh yes, Malcolm, and guess what? Jack has started to eat his vegetables."

"But only carrots and peas," Jack cut in quickly. "I 'ate cabbage I do, and sprouts – *YEEUCK!*"

Malcolm laughed out loud at the little boy's screwed up face, then winked at mum. "In that case, can I gi'em one o' me sweets?" Malcolm would never dream of offering children a sweet without the permission of a responsible adult. He had read too many stories in the newspapers about nasty grown-ups who pretended to be nice, giving presents to children who didn't know they weren't very nice until it was too late. He waited until the young mother nodded and smiled.

"Okay, Malcolm – but only one,"

Malcolm delved into his donkey jacket and brought out a packet of sherbet-lemons. Not the loose ones that come in a jar, stick together and attract bits of hair and fluff in your pocket, no, these were individually wrapped and came in a sealed packet.

"'Ere y'are children," he would say. "An' be sure t'clean yer teeth after or they'll go all yeller!"

"They will, Malcolm, they will," mum assured; the kids nodded eagerly and helped themselves.

"Say goodbye – and thank you, children," said mum.

"Thank you, Malcolm, bye-bye." And with cheeks bulging, little Jack and Rosie would skip off down the road, just ahead of their mother, leaving Malcolm to gaze down the street after them with hands on his hips, shaking his head in wonderment and blinking away a joyful tear. "I dunno," he'd muse, "ruddy kids, eh – lovely, innit?"

Skill with the pooperscooper. Kindness with younger children – and these occasions happened nearly every day, not just now and again. The residents of Suburbiaville Newtown were far too professional, far too artistic and far too posh to worry about things like litter and clean streets. But they would soon complain if they were not maintained to the highest standard. They preferred to leave things of this nature to unimportant people like Malcolm. That was his job after all – and he was so good at it. They would have to leave him a good tip at Christmas. But if they forgot to, Malcolm wouldn't mind – he knew his place in the food-chain – he liked to help.

Oh yes – and then there was the time when Malcolm dashed to the rescue of that elderly lady on the corner of Willowy Lane. The poor woman was standing at the bus stop, searching through her bag for her bus-pass. She must have dropped it somewhere, it couldn't have been stolen, not on Willowy Lane; it was far too idyllic. *Oh no* – she began to weep – she would have to telephone her son, he worked in the city, something to do with banks and finance. *He* would have to get something in for tea; this, also, had happened before and her son was none too happy about it last time. Maybe her son would put her in an old people's home; the thought made her shiver and shake with fear, the stories she had heard about them. *Bbrrr*, it was enough to turn your hair white – again.

Then, along came Malcolm pushing his unwieldy barrow. He saw the elderly lady, saw the tears running down her cheeks, heard her muttering, "Oh no, whatever will I do now?"

"G'mornin' ma'am – what ails thee on such a luvverly mornin'?" he asked. "Can I help yer in any way?" So the old lady told him what the trouble was, told him about that dreadful old people's home. Malcolm could see the lady was almost having a panic attack.

"Please don't you fret, my lovely," Malcolm soothed her, "I'll run yer to town in this." And he removed the forward bin on his barrow – hiding the bin behind a bush, camouflaging it with leaves and twigs because shiny, galvanised, steel dustbins are worth their weight in gold.

"Please my ol' darlin' – sit thee down." He gestured with a dramatic sweep of his arms. A large, empty space was left in front of the barrow. Malcolm helped the elderly lady settle comfortably into it, lean her back against the rear dustbin. Then he pushed the lady to town in comfort and safety. And because they did not have to stop to pick up other passengers, they arrived ten minutes ahead of the bus – and so could choose the *best* food available.

That evening her son, who had quite a sharp temper because he worked so hard, feasted on a banquet and never found out about the bus pass. For Malcolm found it later when he took the lady home and stopped for a cup of tea and a chat. He spotted the pass underneath a pile of unopened mail; the corner was just sticking out beneath it.

Apparently her son had dumped it on the coffee table and had not noticed the pass the night before.

"Well," the old lady said, "they *did* work him very hard indeed at the bank and he couldn't remember everything – poor chap."

Displays of professionalism; acts of kindness towards small children; willingness to help elderly people in their hour of need; and, of course, his clean and smart – some would say suave – appearance endeared the residents of Suburbiaville to Malcolm. Here was a man, they thought, one of the "rank and file" who, despite his lower station and lack of education, was willing to go that extra mile just for them. We deserve it after all – we must remember to give him a tip at Christmas...

Chapter 4

Monday is Only a Weekend Away

Thursday in Suburbiaville was payday. After work all the builders, all the maintenance workers, all the factory hands, the warehouse-men and checkout-girls from the local supermarkets and other public-service workers, would meet up in "The Artisan's Arms" – a local ale-house on the outskirts of the town – to celebrate payday and the oncoming weekend.

Late on a Thursday afternoon was always a noisy affair and sometimes, the celebrations – much to the delight of the landlord and his wife – would often carry on into the early evening. The till would not stop ringing, the fruit machines would not stop swallowing coins and coughing-up the *occasional* jackpot – *very* occasional. Alcohol and meals were served, jokes were told with peals of exaggerated laughter and naughty songs were sung, with bags of enthusiasm but, sadly, not much talent.

After work, Malcolm would pop in for a couple of pints; he liked the feel of the place, the buzz of the workers. Here, he felt, was somewhere that anyone could come to and have a laugh. But on this occasion, he noticed a different atmosphere. The juke-box still played, the fruit machine was still occasionally paying-out and songs were still being sung, things just felt different somehow. It was as though *something* had happened, or was about to happen. And nobody would tell him about it.

"'Allo Geordie!" He saw his mate Geordie at the bar. A giant of a man from Newcastle, one of the drivers from the council works depot. "Where've you been, mate? I 'aven't seen yer fer a good few weeks."

But he seemed different too. "Oh 'ullo Malcy, ol' son – 'ow are ye, mucker? Ah've been away, in 'Umberside on a course, like?" his loud, sing-song accent cut through the din in the bar.

"Oh aye," Malcolm asked conversationally, "What course is that then?"

At this Geordie stuck a finger in his ear and waggled it around. "What's that? Ah canna hear ye in all this racket, mon – we'll talk later. We've gotta new wagon, like – cor, is that the time like?" He glanced at the clock above the bar. "Ah – look mucker. Gorra dash like! See ye later, mon." And he pushed through the crowd in the pub and did not say another word.

That's funny, thought Malcolm, scratching his head, I didn't know Geordie was hard of hearing. He was quite disappointed at his mate's quick get-away. Maybe he's got problems at home, because I know he's got a couple of kids – an' you know what an 'andful *they* can be.

It was time to go home, to clean and maintain his equipment. Oh aye, an' I'll have to pop in to that cycle shop and get some more lubricant – oh yeah, an' some more o' them Sherbet Lemons for the kids...

When he turned up at the depot on Friday – his barrow freshly lubricated, the galvanised bins buffed up and shining like a shilling – Gordon Bartholemew, who would usually greet him with a cheery wave and a patronising, "Good morning, Malcolm," then vanish into his office for the rest of the day, on this particular morning announced that he could not stop, nor would he meet Malcolm's eyes. Pointing at his watch and muttering something about a meeting he had to attend five minutes ago, he disappeared.

Nobody, it seemed, had any time to stop and chat. Those workers who used the staff canteen, the people who would gather in the yard outside after breakfast – the people who'd stop and chat with Malcolm, before starting work – for some reason or other, had to be somewhere else.

"Sorry Malcolm, can't stop, I'm in the middle of an oil-change," a garage mechanic excused himself and hurried away.

"Mornin' Malc. Got a text from Eckerslike upstairs." The Fire Safety Officer raised his eyes. "Would you believe it, all the fire-alarms on the first floor are down." The man was in an awful flap – and he was normally so calm. "Better go and see what's up!"

"Can I 'elp?" asked Malcolm brightly. "I'm I dab 'and with that sort of thing!"

"No – no, it's alright Malcy, better check them out myself, regulations you know – see you later." And he was gone.

Responses like this had Malcolm scratching his head; blimey, I was only offering to 'old his ladder! he thought. Then he went into the main building. Everybody was hard work, typing letters or arranging work schedules, budgets and what have you and so had no time to talk. Some people – and it was quite a small office – pretend they hadn't seen him.

So he went to check the notice-board but found that somebody had taken time to clear it of rotas, memos and other such notes which may have given him some kind of clue. At the end of the corridor were the steps that led up to the first-floor of the management offices and he half thought about climbing them, hammering on the door, demanding: "What the heck have I done? Why won't anybody speak to me – I thought I was well-liked round here!" But he thought better of it. A little disappointed, Malcolm just shrugged his shoulders, none the wiser as to what was amiss and went back on his rounds, thinking: I dunno – sometimes nobody tells yer nothin'... But somehow something was different, he could feel it in the breeze, could smell it in the air.

What our Malcolm did not know was that that fateful Monday morning was looming near. In three days it was going to happen. Only the weekend to go and then it would be here – and everyone but he knew about it. And even if he did, there wasn't anything he could do to stop it. That was *progress*...

Chapter 5

The Future According to Geordie

Eight-thirty on Monday morning: a full *hour* before most council workers used to turn up. It was a beautiful spring day in April, birds were singing in the trees, a milk-float laden with cow-juice and rich-in-vitamin-C fruit drinks whirred along, the milkman whistling cheerfully as he delivered. "Whistling cheerfully" was a condition written in to the milkman's "terms of employment" contract, when he delivered to homes in Willowy Lane. It added, Suburbiaville Newtown council felt, to the lane's blissful nature.

Malcolm had pushed his barrow up the hill to Suburbiaville British Rail station, cleaning in front of every garden gate as he passed. Chatting with any residents he met. Distributing the odd sherbet lemon to any lucky children he met, provided that they had been good – maybe they had eaten all their vegetables the evening before, or had got ten out of ten in a spelling test at school.

Having cleared the waiting-room and platform of paper cups, newspapers, tissues and other travellers' trash he was about to push his unwieldy barrow down the other side of the hill.

It was good to be alive on mornings like these, Malcolm decided, not too cold, not too hot with just the right amount of breeze. He would go out for a stroll with Gisele, that girl from the depot office tonight; they had become friends only recently when they discovered they shared an interest in astronomy. There was a full moon tonight. They would watch it together and, perhaps, have a quick drink. When, hang on, what's that?

... A high-pitched whine – a sort of cross between a distant aeroplane, a herd of angry elephants and a trumpet being blown by an untrained trumpeter – reached his ears. It was as though a hundred, no, maybe *five* hundred household vacuum cleaners had been switched on all at once. With eyes closed tight, he tried to work out using only his ears what the cause of the noise could be. When he opened them again a huge vehicle rolled out of a side-turning, coming to a halt on the side of Willowy Lane, opposite to where he had cleaned, a long way down the street from him.

"What on earth is that?" he wondered aloud. "Crikey – it's gonna take off in a mo…" From where Malcolm stood – about half a mile away – it seemed as though this beast had sprouted wings. But we know different, don't we? Seeming to appear from beneath these wings, four of what looked like wheelie bins on caterpillar tracks trundled out onto the road, two on either side. It looked like four *ugly chicks* had just hatched and were nestling beneath the wings of their *even uglier* mother. Malcolm pushed his barrow nearer to the "All-in-One-Der" to get a better look. As he approached, the "Rubbish Robots" – bursting with nanotechnology – buzzed into life. Breaking formation, escaping from under the wings, these "chicks" became individuals with minds of their own. The droid-bins dived into front gardens, back gardens, driveways, dustbin areas.

Guzzling garden waste. Destroying everyday dirt. Removing rubbish. Purging poo, paint and oil stains from pavements. Breaking down boxes and slurping up semi-solid or gooey stuff directly into their *guts*. Crumpling cardboard and sorting a variety of recyclable materials into categories then storing it out in front of the house to be picked up by the recycling van later. Seeking out any matter that could be described as foreign with their flashing red sensor and, promptly, deporting it, whilst at the same time scrubbing the concrete paths clean with the brushes beneath each robot's tracks, until Willowy Lane looked like an advert in an estate agent's manual. These *droids* seemed to possess an energy that had Malcolm gulping and wondering how, or even if, he would be able to compete with these machines.

Racing around as they scrubbed oil and paint from affected areas, ducking and diving, weaving intricate patterns. These *dust-devils* reminded Malcolm of "The Red Arrows" display team, he had seen on television a couple of times. He watched, his mouth opening and closing in time with the "Jaws" of the "Crusher", as every time a "Rubbish Robot" filled itself up it would belch, and return to be hoisted and emptied into that ever-hungry hopper.

Then the finale: buzzing, bleeping, whizzing and whirling the "Rubbish Robots" returned to the "All-in-One-Der", lining up like hungry schoolchildren in the dinner-queue to be emptied into that ravenous hopper one last time – accompanied by that characteristic, cute "burping" sound. In reality, this final belch was an electrical message to the control-box that this was the final load to be crushed. It would then send orders to "The Crusher" to "continue crushing" and to munch the rubbish into material small enough for the hopper to digest.

The droid wheelie-bins then re-grouped under the outstretched, wing-like, cantilever doors. Maybe, thought Malcolm, whatever these things were were getting their breath back after all that racing around. Then they simply paired off, turned inwards and, from where Malcolm was standing at the other end of Willowy Lane, seemed to disappear into the side of the vehicle under the doors.

The icing was put on the cake when the vast vehicle started forward, the large rolling brush going round and round, constantly turning. It was then dealt with by "The Dirt Disperser", a *new* improvement added by a *whiz-kid* mechanic in the "Motor Transport" (MT) department, at the depot. This device looked like an enlarged industrial vacu-um-cleaner head which was connected to a large suction-pipe and lay, like a basking python, over the roof of the vehicle, and sucked any gritty or sandy waste that the Rubbish Robots may have missed directly into the hopper.

Malcolm struggled to get a grip on what he had just seen. It was unbeliev-able. It was remarkable. Maybe it was remarkably unbelievable or unbelievably remarkable. Who knows – it could have been a bit of both. Cardboard had been crushed. Paper had been shredded. Rubbish removed and the entire area "blitzed". The whole operation had taken minutes. Malcolm was fast *and* efficient, but by the time he had stopped and chatted to everyone, given sherbet lemons to well-behaved children and helped elderly people do whatever they had to do, one street would take a full morning. And that was if he did not spend time polishing the door-numbers on houses; he liked to make sure each number was clean and stood out clearly. That way the postman would be able to read each door-number clearly and deliver the right mail to the right house, another reason Malcolm saw his job as essential. He could not bear the thought that because he did not do his job properly, some poor home-owner may receive mail addressed to somewhere else; the confusion it would cause, the sheer panic.

He pushed his barrow across the street to this great vehicle – what a weird wagon; it's like something out of Doctor Who. Only it's more like Doctor What – Malcolm's mind was working overtime. What are these strange robots? What the heck was going on? The "All-in-One-Der" was ticking over quietly, menacingly.

The sun reflecting on the windows made it impossible see who the driver was, so he rapped on the window sharply. An electrical whirring, the window wound down – PUWEEZZZZ – the whirring stopped.

It was his "mate", Geordie the driver. "Oh 'allo, Malky ol' son – what are ye doin' 'ere, mon? What's up, mucker?" All sweetness and surprise, mixed with a degree of pride and smugness at his new job, as if he was saying, "*I've* been promoted but I'll still talk to you." Clearly, he was not expecting to see Malcolm.

"W-what's goin' on?" stammered Malcolm, confused by this new situation, awestruck by this enormous machine.

"'Aven't yer 'eard mon – we've gan all 'igh-tech," Geordie went on to explain, "Ah've been away on a course learnin' how to drive this beggar. They're phasing yer oot, mon. Malcy ol' son – ah'm afraid yer obsolete, mon!"

Malcolm looked down the street. He had to take his hat off to those droids. They had done a fantastic job, in a fraction of the time. Willowy Lane looked immaculate, clear of rubbish, garden gates closed, gutters swept and vacuumed. Pavements hosed and scrubbed. So quickly, so easily, so efficiently, so effortlessly. But it was all so impersonal, it lacked the human touch. Malcolm just did not know what to say.

"I – I don't know what to say."

"Say what ye like, mon – this is the future," said Geordie matter-of-factly. He grimaced and hunched his shoulders. "Yerra thing o' the past noo!" He leaned out the cab window, covering his mouth with his hand so that only Malcolm could hear. "If Ah was you, Malcy ol' son, Ah wuild wait till Monday, like. An' gan an' see that feller, Eckerslike, like. He'll be able tea tell yer what's 'appenin', like!"

Malcolm could not believe it. After all the years of dedication. After all his hard work and professionalism. The council wanted simply to oust him and in his place put mindless machines. And nobody had said anything to him about it.

So that was why no-one had any time to stop and chat on Friday...

This made Malcolm angry – very angry indeed. But he didn't lose his temper; in his practised country drawl he said, "Oh-arr, we'll just 'ave to see about that – won't we?" He pointed Belinda, his barrow, in the direction of the council depot, and set off at a brisk pace. But when he got there he found them locked up and empty, the administration staff, i.e. Mister Bartholemew, was at some kind of administrative meeting in London and had taken his secretary Gisele with him to take the minutes. Mr Eckerslike was on the golf-course, meeting *important people* at the nineteenth hole, buying huge rounds of drinks and recruiting sponsors for his nomination for the position of Lord Mayor of Suburbiaville in the Mayoral Elections taking place during the following summer. He would claim the money he spent buying those drinks back from expenses. Our Willy would never be short of a few quid. All the other workers, who would hang around the yard, all had business elsewhere and were "too busy to stop and chat" so Malcolm was none the wiser for his visit to the depot.

In the end, his head buzzing with questions, he returned home to his flat on the other side of town and quelled his frustrations alone in his garden shed, polishing his dustbins, cleaning and lubricating his barrow. Then, after selecting a fresh shirt and tie for the coming Monday, he went to bed early with an uneasy feeling – *what was going on?*

Chapter 6

Thunderclouds in the Office

Mister Bartholemew looked out of the window of his tiny office and frowned. Something about the man standing in the yard outside intrigued him. He was sure, well, almost definitely sure that he had seen this man before. The way he stood, proud, smart with an almost military bearing; he stood out from other workers in the yard, smarter, more crisply dressed. Really, he found his presence quite unnerving, menacing even. It did not occur to him that he bumped into this man most mornings during the working week. He asked his secretary, Gisele.

"Miss Thunderhosen – who is that that extremely well-turned out individual standing outside in the yard?"

"Mein Fuehrer – das ist Malkolm, vun of your street cleanink operatiffs – he has been standink out zhere since eight-thirty zis mornink!"

"Good heavens. How do you know that? These offices don't open until nine-thirty which means that you do not have to come in until nine o'clock sharp."

"Mein Fuhrer – ve ist bekomink ver' klose friends – und ve ist schtayink up until twelve o'clock last night vatching der moon und der tvinklink stars, und holdink der hands." Her voice softened and rose an octave as Gisele continued in pidgin English mixed with her own guttural German, "Ah, it vos wunderbah – und Malky ist such a gentlemann." Again her tone changed, she became quite cross indeed, "*However* last nacht he said he vould haff to be krying off und get his head down early because he ist gettink up ver' ver' early in der morgen so he could catch you. He says you ist runnink away all der *flippink* time – humph!"

Mister Bartholemew looked through his tiny office window and scratched his head. Deep in thought, he ran his index finger under his lower lip. "Hmmm – I must say he doesn't look very happy." Malcolm was standing against the far wall, almost expressionless but for a fixed jaw and the traces of an angry frown on his forehead.

"Mein Fuehrer – he zinks you vant to giff him der old heave-ho."

"So he knows then?"

"Jawohl, mein Fuehrer. I vould say he has der kleine inkling – und I must say vas a vay to be finding out!" Gisele's voice softened again. She swallowed, fighting back a tear or two. "Mein poor kleine Malky!"

"Yes – but Gisele, it isn't my fault, I – I just couldn't bring myself to tell him. Just look at him out there – he's so smart, suave even. So smooth and efficient. So – so, what's the word, Gisele?"

"Konscientious – mein Fuehrer?"

"Yes conscientious – that's it. He is just so conscientious that I couldn't bring myself to tell him. He's so dependable, is Malcolm. Out there in all weathers. Come rain or shine – and he's so clean and well-groomed. *Ahem.*" Mister Bartholemew stopped dead; he was beginning to go on a bit. "But I'll have to break it to him gently somehow. Soften the blow. You know, sweeten the bitter pill." Mister Bartholemew was really dreading this confrontation, ever since he had received that directive, that order from *upstairs* to "lay off" most of the street cleaning staff. Suddenly he had a "brilliant" idea. "I know, I'll offer him the depot gardening vacancy."

"Vas?" Gisele scoffed, "Zhose two

scrappy liddle lawns und ein vindow-box
– *poo!* Meine Malky ist ein skilled artist.
Und anyvay das ist only two morninks
verk a veek!" A sharp intake of breath.
Gas escaped from somewhere in Gisele's
head. She let fly. "Vhy are you not standink up to der management dumkopfs?
I zink you are ein gross koward –" and
she added in a mocking tone, "Like der
kowardly kowardly kustard!"

Mister Bartholemew was not used to
being spoken to like this, not by his secretary anyway; who did she think she was?
His tone sharpened. "Look Miss Thunderhosen – Mister Eckerslike said, *make
cuts* and if Mister Eckerslike says, *make
cuts,* we make cuts. *Understand?* And –
tough luck my old darling – Malcolm is
one of those cuts we have to make! He's
the boss is Mister Eckerslike. And what
Mister Eckerslike wants, Mister Eckerslike gets – ooohh he's a great man."
Meaning that it was in Mister Eckerslike's power to fire him if he disagreed
too often. So Gordon Bartholemew just
gritted his teeth and nodded his head
whenever Willy Eckerslike tried out a
new idea on him. Mister Bartholemew
knew only too well what fate befell those
who opposed the Managing Director of
Suburbiaville council.

That outburst took a lot out of Mr Bartholemew. He sat down, wheezing and
out of breath; his therapist had told him

before not to get so excited. Dismissing or disciplining staff was a part of his job that he loathed. Council works managers were the *mouth pieces* of the Managing Directors and the Managing Director in this council was Mister Willy Eckerslike. In other words, Mister Eckerslike could hire and fire who he liked. The workers never saw him. He just wrote a little note, a directive, and sent it downstairs to Mister Bartholemew. And Mister Bartholemew implemented his instructions. Poor old Gordon fired the bullets that Willy loaded into the gun.

When he got his breath back Mister Bartholemew barked sharply, using as much authority as he could muster – which wasn't very much, "Miss Thunderhosen – show him in!"

Gisele shrugged and was about to say something back when Mister Bartholemew raised a hand for silence then added a sly afterthought, with aloofness: "I think one should remember, Miss Thunderhosen, that if it wasn't for Suburbiaville council's willingness to employ and house you, one may find oneself back in East Germany where one belongs...

"It could quite easily withdraw that support we so generously afforded you in your hour of need – then where would you be?"

Gisele did not know what to say. Mr Bartholemew, or rather the *big-wigs* at

Suburbiaville council, held the trump card. She turned, clicked her heels together, and through the open window bellowed sweetly, gently. "Koo-ee, Malky darlink – Herr Bartholemew vill see you noww!!!"

The windows were still rattling in their frames when Malcolm nodded his head, tucked his broom under his arm and marched quickly, with the hint of a swagger, into the council building. He came to a smart, almost military halt outside Mister Bartholemew's door, and knocked sharply on the door three times.

"Yes – who is it?" Mister Bartholemew asked through the door – as if he didn't know.

"Mister Bartholemew sir, it is I, sir, Malcolm – one of your street cleaners."

Footsteps sounded inside, the door was wrenched open. "Malc my old mate – don't mind if I call you Malc – do you?" Mister Bartholemew was wearing the sort of smile that kills at twenty paces. "Come in – come in. Sit down, relax – would you like anything? Tea, coffee – you will call me Gordon, won't you. All my friends call me Gordon." The truth was, that in all his years as Works Manager, nobody had called him Gordon. He went on.

"Now I gathered you wanted to see me." He smiled again, putting on his *caring employer* mask.

"No thankee, Mister Bartholemew, sir, I'd rather call 'ee Mister Bartholemew, sir – if y'don't mind, like. Gives me a sense of where I fit in."

"As you wish, as you wish, er, Malc. I must admit I do rather enjoy being called sir." The truth was that in the same number of years nobody had called Mister Bartholemew "sir" either. He went on, "Now I understand you have a problem – in what way can I help?"

Malcolm took a deep breath. "Well, Mister Bartholemew sir, it's like this: I'm out there this mornin' doin' me rounds like. An' just when I gets 'alfway round like, this 'uge – no – it was gigantic – no it was *enormous* – gert wagon pulls up. An' all these robots come out the side like. An' then they starts emptyin' bins, sweepin' up, 'ooverin' up dirt an' dust – an' they only got one eye – un'oly it was, Mister Bartholemew sir... un'oly..." He shuddered, then continued, "So there I am like, wonderin' what the thunderin' eck's goin' on like. An' then I sees Geordie – the driver like. An' 'e tells me you've gone all 'igh tech like. 'E's bin on a course an' I'm obsolete – no – what did 'e call it – a thing o' the past – well one o' the two. Either way I'm out of a job – well it just ain't fair, Mister Bartholemew sir. It just ain't. An' then 'e just drives off – wiv that big roller in the front goin' round an' round..."

Mister Bartholemew rose from behind his desk and walked over to where Malcolm stood, quaking with frustration – remember, it was only a tiny office, so Mister Bartholemew almost fell over Malcolm as he did – and gently placed an arm around his shoulders, drawing him into a brotherly embrace. "Come now Malc, my old mate – how long have we been friends?"

Malcolm writhed in the embrace – he did not like this at all – and answered, "Well sir, Mister Bartholemew sir. Ever since you put your arm round me and I can't say I'm that 'appy about it either, Mister Bartholemew sir. A bit familiar don't you think – Mister Bartholemew sir?"

Mister Bartholemew dropped his arm. This was going to be harder than he thought. He sighed loudly and tried to put his hands on his hips; unfortunately his arms were too long and thin and the office was so small that this proved quite impossible, so he put them in his pockets. "Come now, MALC my old – *ah* – chum, there really is no cause for alarm – *ahem!*" He cleared his throat. "So you've met our new *Rubbish Robots* – a bit scary eh?" He forced a laugh, nudging Malcolm with an elbow, his *right* elbow, as there wasn't enough room to turn round and nudge him with the left, "Aha – aha – ha – ha – haa!"

No reaction, Malcolm failed to see any humour in the remark. "Oh well," commented Mister Bartholemew and came straight to the point. "The thing is Malc, my old pal, we at Suburbiaville Council…" Meaning the big-wigs on the floor above, Mr Bartholemew was only an office Dogsbody after all, Willy Eckerslike's *whipping-boy*, "…Have found it necessary to *revamp* our highway maintenance service – ah, um – particularly our street cleaning service, am I going too fast?"

"No – no, Mr. Bartholemew, sir. I follow yer."

"To bring us in line or to possibly compete with – er, as it were – our European neighbours. And management – and, er, um – I really must agree, I think that – er - the best way forward is to replace that element of human frailty, risk – call it what you will – with – um, ah – mechanical superiority." Mr Bartholemew's voice rose as he put the icing on the cake. "And the beautiful part about all this is that we don't have to pay them a penny, whereas we pay you…" Mr Bartholemew snatched a notebook from his desk. Then he snatched a figure out of the air and scribbled it down, shoving it under Malcolm's nose. Malcolm gasped.

"But Mr Bartholemew, you don't pay me anything like…"

"Sssshh – now Malc, my old chum – bit

of creative book-keeping there, that's all that is. How do you think I can afford to take Missus Bartholemew to Majorca twice a year?"

"But Mister Bartholemew sir, *mechanical superiority*, how can you say that... They're like them dalek-wosnames on 'Doctor Who' – always bleeping an' buzzin' – I point-blank refuse to be replaced by a rabble of rowdy robots. An'– an'..." Malcolm's voice trailed off into a hoarse whisper; as he ran out of breath his voice became weaker. "You can't get rid o' me, Mister Bartholemew sir, I'm an artist, I am – a guru of the kerb and gutter..."

"Yes, I agree, Malcolm, but you're not a very quick one, are you? Not compared to our robots. And that's the *buzz-word* here. We need speed, *baby*. Super, zippy-fast action man. The kind that will put us in line with our European counterparts. Plus – and I think I touched on this beforehand – we don't have to pay them any money." Mister Bartholemew gestured, if that was possible given the size of the office, towards the yard. The droids, lined up in the middle of the yard, silent and unmoving, were visible through the office window. Sunlight reflected on the plates bearing their identification numbers: RR: 1, RR: 2, RR: 3, and RR: 4.

Malcolm glared through the window

at them – he could imagine them laughing, or in any case burping at him. He turned to Mister Bartholemew. "So that's it then, eh? I'm on the scrapheap. It's *Goodbye Charlie* fer ol' Malcy..."

"Now, now Malcolm – nobody is trying to get rid of you," soothed Mister Bartholemew – poor chap, he wasn't all bad, just a snivelling coward, that's all. And he could not bear the thought of crossing Willy Eckerslike and losing his own job; he needed the money because Missus Bartholemew had expensive tastes, you know, she did like her holidays in Majorca.

"Have you ever considered a career in horticulture?" he suggested. "Now *there's* something – um – more worthy of a man with your talents, requires skill, your kind of attention to detail. Fresh air – the smell of the earth. Good hard work. Oh – those halcyon days of summer, eh? – and you could have your pick of fresh flowers and plants. You could even start a vegetable garden. And you get your very own 'Head Gardener' badge. Of course..." Mr Bartholemew lowered his voice, "...you would have to retrain, attend technical college." Then in almost a whisper, "And there is the small cut in wages to consider but you wouldn't have to work such long hours..."

Malcolm shook his head, "Mister Bartholemew, sir. You can't do this to me.

You just can't I've been a street cleaner all me workin' life – that's nigh on 27 years, you know? My father was a street-cleaner, an' his father, an' his father an' then o' course there's 'is father and 'is father's father. 'Oo do you think piled up all them stones so neatly at Stone'enge. An' it was one o' my forefathers who cleared up all those bows an' arrows an' stuff after the battle of 'Astings. Blimey, Mister Bartholemew, sir. I ain't no gardener, sir..."

About then Mister Bartholemew's temper flared, not because he was angry at Malcolm but because of the thought that he was dismissing a faithful worker. And why? Because he had been told to, that is why.

Oh well – he'd tried the softly-softly approach; no more mister nice guy. "Now look Malcolm, I've tried be gentle about this. I've tried to lessen the shock – I've even offered you another – *ah* – position to replace your former one. And what have you done in return? Let me tell you – you've thrown it all back my face, that's what. Don't bother coming in tomorrow, or the next day or the day after that because there isn't anything for you to do. In fact, we never want to see you again, is that clear?"

Then Mister Bartholemew switched moods again from angry and exasperated to crisp and businesslike. His nerves would never stand-up to all these mood-swings. "Your P45 and any severance pay will be sent to you in the post..."

Distant thunder clouds began to roll and a lightning bolt flashed round the room as Mister Bartholemew added darkly, gravely, "And may God have mercy on your soul. Close the door on your way out. *Thankyop!*"

That was it. Malcolm's world collapsed. It was as though the rug had been pulled out from under him. It was as though two rugs had been pulled out from under him.

As he trudged through the yard he looked up at the first-floor windows; the sun's reflection had turned them into mirrors. Behind those mirrors dark forces were at work. Forces that sought to take the efforts of hard working human beings, like Malcolm, and replace them with the precision of mindless machines, in an attempt to save money.

Gisele watched through the window as her "liddle" Malky trudged through the gates of the council depot – a broken man. She did not like this at all. Since they had been going out *stargazing* and *moon-watching* together, she had become more and more attracted to this chap. She could feel his pain. And that hurt. Her Malky was always so slick, so forth-right and proud. Her Malky was always so clean and smart – with a bit more crackle than the average live wire. That was the Malcolm who had practically marched into the office this morning. But it wasn't the Malcolm who slouched out of the depot gates, his head down – *his hands in his pockets...*

Chapter 7

Malcolm's Wallow/
Gisele's Despair

So that was that then. At forty-three years of age, that's only three years after when life begins for most people, and faced with year upon year of unemployment, Malcolm found himself on the scrapheap. Mere flotsam on the sea of life. It did not take very long at all for him to begin to feel worthless.

Depression is a terrible thing, you know, and it went hand in hand with that feeling of worthlessness; he did not feel as though he mattered anymore and nothing else did either.

Suburbiaville Town Council did not waste much time repossessing his unwieldy barrow but it wasn't done openly during the day, and he was not presented with the "chitty" he signed in exchange for it all those years ago. Instead Mister Eckerslike sent a couple of *heavies* round to Malcolm's shed; well, one was heavy, the other was a bit thin and scrawny but just as violent. And told them to, "Gerrit o'er t'town's Museum of Antiquities!" Where it was displayed on a podium with a plaque which read: "Tools of the street cleaner before the great days of total mechanisation."

"...And if that Tilsley feller gets in t'way gi' 'im a thick ear – yer 'ave my permission to gi' 'im a good thumpin', I said yer 'ave..." But Willy did not have to repeat himself; the two hoodlums were relishing a bit of breaking and entering with the added possibility of a bit of violence. Luckily Malcolm had the television volume turned up full blast watching an Australian soap opera until he felt quite ill. He did not hear the yobbos break into his shed or who knows what would have happened.

Along with that barrow, Eckerslike's *heavies* had managed to gain possession of his trusty pooperscooper, Malcolm's prize possession. Normally the device would have been kept under lock and key in the safety of Malcolm's flat, but following his abrupt dismissal, feeling rejected and empty of all other emotions he had left it in its *quick-release* compartment on the barrow, left the shed door unlocked and gone to watch the Aussie soap opera on television. This made him even more depressed so when the credits came up, he sat there transfixed and sulked for days.

As well as the idyllic Willowy Lane, the surrounding area and Suburbiaville's less desirable areas there was, too, the totally undesirable area. This area was a huge, so far undeveloped piece of land on the far reaches of the town. It was the home of undesirables, down-and-outs and those who were down on their luck or those who had, somehow, fallen foul of society. It was the sort of place that parents of Willowy Lane told their children to avoid. And the sort of place that children went to for "a dare".

This was the place where local factories, small time businesses and a couple of larger concerns could come and "fly-tip" their rubbish, ditch their dangerous chemicals, without fear of being caught and prosecuted. The police would occasionally send a squad car to the area just to maintain a "police presence" but it never hung around for very long. Come on, we all know these places exist. It was to this place that Malcolm was, in his depressed state, drawn. Here he felt safe. Here nobody knew him. Here he was nobody – just another of life's failures who nobody wanted.

And it was here he started *drinking* and

not just a couple of celebratory pints of beer on pay day either. Malcolm never did receive any severance pay from the council, because he had quit his flat the postman could not obtain a signature for the recorded delivery and so had return the package unopened to the sender. Eventually it came into the possession of Mister Willy Eckerslike who took it upstairs to his office, put it in a bottom drawer and locked it. He was not about to be accused of withholding a man's pay, not him. Not the future Mayor of Suburbiaville.

Having received no pay Malcolm had no money and so could not afford buy alcohol, so when he finished the bottle of Cinzano from the drinks cabinet in his flat, which he had originally bought for when Gisele visited on Christmas day, he started to drink the kind of drink that wasn't supposed to be drank – metal polish, shoe conditioner, methylated spirits. Anything he could find that had been dumped on that wasteland. It did not taste very nice and you had to dilute it with rain water because if you drank it straight down and unmixed, it made your vision go all zig-zaggy and in the end you could not see a thing.

For just over a fortnight this was Malcolm's daily routine: he'd awake after flaking out after an evening of binging on whatever solvent he could find. You name it: shoe conditioner, adhesive, metal polish – anything with a kick in it, and he'd just stare blankly into space until a black, unconscious state overcame him. Then, hours later, daylight would filter into his head, and off he would go on a tour of skips and dustbins to stock up for the next evening. Malcolm was on the road to ruin and he knew it. How many other famous artists have taken this path and were unable to return?

But it had the effect of making you forget, it dulled the awful memory of his dismissal. And forgetting is exactly what Malcolm wanted to do. He wanted to forget that he could have once had a career in medicine. Wanted to forget his smart and dapper appearance, wanted to forget his skill and dexterity with the pooperscooper. The elderly ladies he had helped in their hour of need and his special relationship with mothers and their children. And it hurt him badly to think about Gisele and the close relationship he thought they were forming – she would not want to know him now.

Even the local pooches that, out of respect for Malcolm's hard work, did their business in the gutter, would now leave their "calling cards" heaped in unsightly steaming mounds on the pavement. And there they remained, waiting to engulf the shoe of any unaware pedestrian or to ruin the businessman's shiny new footwear. For the "All-in-One-Der" did not begin its daily round until eleven o'clock and residents of Suburbiaville Newtown, especially the rich and famous folk of Willowy Lane, were up and at work long before that doing what rich people do best – making money.

During the next couple of weeks "doggy doos" became such a problem that many a well-shod city gent had taken to wearing trainers to work and carrying their more expensive footwear to work. One of questions raised in *Prime Minister's Question Time* in the House of Commons and aired on BBC TV was: "What is to be done about the doggy-doos in Suburbiaville?"

Sometimes Malcolm would go to the town centre and sit by the fountain, near the duck pond, and have breakfast with the ducks. But when the ducks began to realise that Malcolm was really only interested in the stale crusts of bread people would scatter for them, they took those crusts over to the island in the middle of the pond where they could enjoy them in peace. He would sit on a bench at the water's edge, trying to remember how it had been in the "good old days" but he couldn't, his brain had become *addled*, befuddled by too many chemicals. On one of these occasions he bumped, or rather stumbled, into a young mother taking her two young children to school.

"Oof – oh – er sorry me darling!" But to himself he was thinking, *Perishin' mothers, bloomin' kids – why don't yer watch where yer going?*

"Pardon me!" The young mum excused herself. "Jack! Rosie! Hurry up now, we don't want to be late for school!"

"Who was that nasty man, Mummy?" asked Rosie.

"I don't know, darling, but I *never* want you to speak to people like that – and don't let them breathe on you."

"Yeah, Mum, who was 'e? And where's Malcolm? He was a nice, clean man wasn't he mum?" Jack wanted to know where his friend with the twinkle in his eye had gone. And more importantly, he wanted to know what had happened to his early morning sherbet lemon.

The young mother stopped dead in her tracks, crossed her fingers and told a white lie. "Children, Malcolm has gone away – a long way away."

"Yeah but Mum," Jack would not let the subject drop, "he *is* coming back – isn't he, Mum?" And tears began to well in Rosie's eyes.

Crossing her fingers even tighter, Mum said, "Darling children, I honestly couldn't tell you – now come along or we'll be late for school." And she hurried the kids off to school, but she had an idea of the fate that had befallen Malcolm – that tramp who had just bumped into her looked rather familiar. She hoped she was wrong, but mums are not wrong very often, are they?

Without Malcolm's barrow, there was no longer an unofficial transport route to the town; one or two elderly ladies felt threatened by the thought of going into an old peoples' home because they could not provide their hard-working sons with an evening meal. This was a hot topic at the local O.A.P. day-centre and many clients felt they had nowhere to turn.

But in his bleary drunken state Malcolm had forgotten this. He had forgotten that because of him people could walk to work in safety. He had forgotten that he had once been the scourge of many a pooch, had forgotten his special relationship with mothers and their young children. Had forgotten about his smart turn-out and his reputation for public service above and beyond the call of duty. And worse than that he had forgotten about Gisele.

But Gisele hadn't forgotten about him and how special she felt when in his company, be it in the works depot yard, or when they sat together having a couple of drinks after an evening "Vatching der moon", Malcolm was always such a gentleman. Always smart, always polite, a cut above the rest, he did not swear or smoke and never lost his temper. He always listened to her, was interested in what she had to say and would help her pronounce things when she found them hard to say.

She was proud to be Malcolm's girl-friend, although as an ex-asylum seeker did not expect to become his wife; that was hoping for too much.

It was as though Malcolm had just disappeared and Gisele determined to find out what had happened to her man. During that fortnight she would spend every evening after work searching everywhere for her man. But Malcolm was nowhere to be found. She went to his flat and knocked. No answer. Then she bent down, lifted the letter-box and bellowed softly, sweetly.

"KOO-EE – MALKY LEIBSHON! ZHERE IST EIN FULL MOON TONIGHT. ARE YOU KOMINK OUT TO VATCH IT MIT ME?"

Still no answer. Her invitation was met by the low howl of a prairie wind, as the door swung into an empty hall-way. There was nobody at home. A worried Gisele searched around the flat but found nothing, no note. Malcolm's shirts were still on their hangers, his ties still on the rack. Gisele exclaimed, "MEIN GOTT IN HIMMEL!" Frowned, deep in thought. Then stroked an imaginary beard, put her best foot forward and went in search of her man, calling as she went, "MALKY DARLINK! KOMMEN SIE BITTE!" And, "VHERE ARE YOU. DO NOT BE RUNNINK AVAY – I LUFF YOU UND NEED YOU. YOU IST MAKINK ME BE KRYINK – BOO-HOO (sniff) BOO-HOO (sniff)!" And things like that, but all to no avail. She could *not* find Malcolm. She visited again and made another last-ditch appeal, "OH MALKY LIEBE SHON – VHERE IST YOU UND VAS IST HAPPENINK TO OUR STEADILY GROWINK RELATIONSHIP!" But things had not changed except that she found a couple of families of rats had moved into the flat, attracted by the stale food in the larder.

In the end, loneliness, despair or desperation – maybe all three – drove Gisele into the arms of a lollipop-man. One morning she was trudging wearily to work, after yet another fruitless night searching when she passed the man leaning on his pole on the other side of the school-crossing. The man nodded and smiled. She just stared at him blankly and... *"BOO HOO! (sniff) BOO-HOO! (sniff)..."* started crying.

"Whatever's wrong, my old darling?" The man walked across to her – when the road was clear.

Then the flood gates opened. Gisele told him, in between sniffs and gasps. "URRHURR (sniffle) IT IST MEINE KLEINE MALKY (gasp) HE IST EIN – NEIN – HE IST "DER" STREET CLEANER UND DER KOUNCIL IST DISMISSINK HIM BECAUSE ZHEY HAFF ZHIS NEW KONTRAPTION CALLED DER 'ALL-IN-VUN-DER' UND SAY HE IST NOT KLEAN-INK DER STRASSE FAST ENOUGH!" Gisele was panicking now, working her-self into a right old state, choking and coughing as she tried to get her breath. "UND SO – ALL DER TIME – MEINE KLEINE MALKY IST BEKOMMINK VER' VER' DEPRESSED UND HE HAS DESERTED ME – UND ZHERE IST EIN FULL MOON TONIGHT – UND I HAFF NOVUN TO VATCH IT WITH – BOO-HOO – URR!"

"That's alright darlin', I'll watch 'der moon' wiv yer!" The lollipop-man leant his pole against the school fence and put his arm around Gisele.

"Okay!" Gisele dried her eyes and blew her nose. "But be keepink your handz to yourself – ya?"

Oh no! Had Gisele found somebody else? Did this mark the end for Malcolm and Gisele's strengthening relationship? Was this rosebud of togetherness about to whither and die before it had flow-ered? But let's not get ahead of ourselves;

76

there may yet be a happy ending in these pages.

Suburbiaville was, in reality, only a small town. It was more or less like a village with a great big main road running through. Alongside that road ran the village grapevine. In these small towns, news travels fast. Gossip travels even faster. It did not take very long for news of Gisele's new boyfriend to reach Malcolm's ears through gossip.

What is usually called *smalltalk*, you know, tittle-tattle and meaningless gossip on the streets of Suburbiaville, sometimes, drifted on the wind and reached *Badlands*. Often the news would be brought in by someone who was new to that desolate area. Maybe a millionaire had recently gone bankrupt, taken up residence there and had brought "hot news" of the outside world with them. This is how Malcolm found out about this lollipop-man. One day a recently bankrupted oil tycoon drifted into *Badlands,* bringing with him news of this "brilliant, snappily dressed, very dapper street cleaner" who had been chucked out of his job "'cos the council has gone all mechanised".

Unfortunately for Malcolm the oil tycoon told him himself for he had no idea who Malcolm was, otherwise he may have used a little tact and spared his feelings.

"Oh GODDAMIT! I'm real sorry!" The tycoon, a former oil-baron from Texas apologised when Malcolm told him that he was the "Guy" that this tycoon spoke of.

"Ah had no idea – Ah have one *hellova* big mouth!"

"That's alright!" Malcolm assured him. "You weren't to know that I am he!" And offered the tycoon a swig from his paraffin bottle, which the man declined, saying that he had not sunk that low yet.

But that news was the last straw for Malcolm. He spent the remainder of that week – even though it was only Tuesday morning – wallowing in self pity, still destroying himself with solvents, still staring blankly into space – when he was conscious. No wonder Gisele could not find him; but she would not give up. And here's another one: meanwhile, Malcolm was getting worse. Much worse, drinking more and more hazardous substances, getting worse and worse; deteriorating fast...

One day the huddled figure of a crazed and drunken vagabond was removed from a park bench in the town park. The Residents of Suburbiaville did not like things like ill people, old people, the disabled or vagabonds to be seen by visitors to the town. They felt it may cause a drop in house prices. So a unit of specially trained paramedics was sent out every other Saturday, in a special ambulance, to areas such as the town park and other public areas, to clear it of tramps and low-lifes. The "low-life" in question this time was Malcolm.

He had just woken from another solvent-fuelled bender and had just started searching the public-trash cans for food, to soak up his liquid diet. Who knows? Maybe he would discover a discarded hamburger, party-goers and evening workers did throw away the most amazing things and today he was feeling lucky.

"Look Phil – there's one!" said the paramedic to his driver, pointing at the figure of Malcolm hunched over the waste bin so that it looked as though he was trying to fit his head into it.

"Seen him, Dave, let's pick him up." The ambulance screeched to a halt, the rear doors flew open as Phil leapt out. "Come along now, sir! Let's get you in the warm with a nice cup of tea!"

"But I don't want a *nice* cup o' flippin' tea." Malcolm had found a half-eaten "Giant-Mac" meal and was just about to tuck into it when the medics arrived. "I'm nothing, me – why don't you mind your own... Mere flotsam I am... HIC! OOER! OH NO!" But Malcolm had become yet another victim of too much too soon, and landed flat on his back covered in burger-relish.

"...And better bring a stretcher Dave –

reckon we'll need it!"

For a full hour the two worked on Malcolm's prone figure. Things looked very dicey indeed. But in the end Dave called, "Right Phil – he's breathing a bit more regular – let's get him loaded up, *quickly!*" And in no time at all, the two men had him on a stretcher, hooked up to a drip-feed and were hurtling through the streets, in the direction of Suburbia-ville General Hospital.

Hours later an unconscious Malcolm was transferred from emergency to a recovery ward, where he remained unconscious for days on end.

Chapter 8

A Little Dice with Death

"Ooh Gladys, did you read in the 'Siren' last week about that feller they picked up in the park?"

"You mean the one with..."

"No, not 'im – that feller 'oo did himself in on all that methylated spirit and metal polish and whatnot and stuff like that!" The lady, still dressed in her apron bearing the logo "Suburbiaville Council Domestic Services" with a duster and rubber gloves pushed into the pouch-pocket, lowered her voice and spoke in a hushed tone to her friend. "You know, that one who frightened all them ducks at the town park. Well, Dorrie, that woman in the Co-op told me he was with that girl up at the depot offices – well, they split up, see. An' *he* went doo-lally, see. Started drinking all sorts o' muck."

"Oh him, yeahss!" Dorrie folded her arms and blew out through her cheeks. "Four *hours* they were pumping out his stomach, well that's what I heard anyway. What was his name, Marcus? Milton? Something like that. O' course I blame the council."

"Oh yeah, Dorrie, why's that luvvy?"

"Well, Glad, it stands to reason, doesn't it? He was a *council* street cleaner wasn't he?"

"Was 'e now?" Gladys was shocked and held a hand to her brow.

"Yeahss!" continued Dorrie, "and they say he was a dapper young man!"

"Do they now?" A sharp intake of breath – Gladys was in awe.

"Yeahss – and the council have gone all high-tech haven't they? They're sacking all the street cleaners and using robots instead – o'course I blame that Eckers-like bloke."

"Why's that then, Dorrie?"

"Well – they say he wants to be the next Mayor. Don't they? And you've got to blame someone, it's *always someone's* fault."

One morning, after another evening searching fruitlessly for her "liddle Malky", a tired, beaten Gisele – *oh, she could not go on much longer* – was trudging wearily to work. Usually she undertook the journey with a spring in her step but ever since she watched Malcolm trudge out of the depot gates and, or so it seemed, out of her life, Gisele's energy levels had dropped to an all-time low. . She had learned to speak English by listening to other people talk and so, could not help but tune into the ladies' conversation.

"Ah – vas ist das?" She could not be she sure she had heard correctly so she listened a bit harder. Then, "Das zounds like mein liddle Malky!" She hitched up her skirt and sprinted girlishly towards the hospital, with new hope surging in her breast.

"Entschuldigen sich bitte – *PUFF! PANT!* – I am lookink for mein klein Malky – *PANT! PUFF!* – but kan I find himm? Nein – I kannot. I am lookink for him here, zhere und everyvhere but he ist novhere to be found. So I am thinking I *am losink himm forever* – HUFF! PUFF! - But zhen I am overhearink zhese two ladies talking about zhis 'dapper jungen man' who ist being picked up und taken to der krankenhaus und zhen I am thinkink that zounds like mein liddle Malky!"

Twenty minutes later Gisele stood in the reception of Suburbiaville General Hospital, having knocked the security senseless after he had attempted to find out the reason for her visiting the hospital outside of visiting hours - silly man.

Emergency reception staff were summoned to take him, unconscious, to the casualty department.

"Yes madam." The man on reception rose quickly from his desk and, brandishing a notebook and pen, ran over to meet her and get a few details... "And how many 'Ds' in *liddle*?"

"*DONNER UND BLITZEN!* You ist vasteing mein time!" Gisele shoulder-barged the man out of the way and the Emergency Reception Team were called again to take another member of the administration team to casualty.

However, Gisele need not have asked directions because – as in all good love-stories – love lit the way and she followed that light all the way to the recovery ward, where Malcolm now lay in bed, watching a day-time documentary on the ward's television, his expression empty, his eyes even emptier.

"Koo-ee Malky darlink!" Gisele enquired around the ward in a hushed whisper. No response – so she enquired a little louder and patients with hearing-aids switched them off. KOO-EE MALKY LIEBE SHON, VHERE ARE YOU? I AM LOOKINK FOR YOU EVERYVHERE. BUT YOU ARE NOVHERE, SO ZEN I AM LOOKINK IN HERE, MIT I SCHTILL KANNOT FIND YOU UND SO I AM KRYINK VER' VER' MUCH! *PLEASE* BE HERE!"

Tears were, once again, beginning to form in Gisele's already watery eyes as they scanned the ward: nothing. Then, on the last sweep of the beds: "AH SO *ZHERE* YOU ARE! I AM LOOKINK ALL OVER FOR YOU UND VHERE ARE YOU. I VILL TELL YOU. YOU ARE IN HERE. *UND VAS IST YOU DOINK.* YOU IST VALLOWING IN YOUR OWN PITY DAS IST VAS YOU ARE DOINK!" There was a brief pause while Gisele got her breath back. The windows stopped rattling in their frames. The walls no longer shook. Then panes of glass began to crack. Plaster began to crumble from the walls. "UND MEIN GOTT! VAS HAVE YOU BEEN DOINK YOU ARE SO SKINNY MIT DER RIBS LIKE EIN GLOCKENSPIEL – YOU IST VASTE-ING AVAY!"

She was right, now he no longer needed that extra bit of bulk to his shoulders to move his unwieldy barrow around with skill and dexterity, those muscles were no longer there. And in their place bones were beginning to push to the surface of his skin. Instead of being a bit of a hunk, he was on the road to becoming a piece of junk.

Malcolm's eyes looked up from the set. "Gisele – it's you innit, what are you doin' here?"

"I haff kommen to wrench you from der depths of despair. Und to re-kindle a liddle leibe in das broken heart of yours."

"Forget it darlin'. I've 'ad it, I 'ave – mere flotsam on the sea of life – that's me..."

"Nein, *nein* Malky do not be sayink das. I do not zink you am ein ham float-ink in der sea; vas ist zis mere ham you ist speaking of?" A puzzled look.

"No – no Gise. You don't understand." Good old Malcolm, true to form, from his sickbed he was still trying to correct Gisele's pidgin English, even when he could see no future in their relationship. Now *that* is love for you, "Flotsam, I said. Flotsam – it's about shipwrecks, things that float about in the sea and stuff like that."

"Oh!" said Gisele, glad to have gained a little knowledge from this difficult situation but still worried at the thought of losing her man. She still looked puzzled as Malcolm went on.

"Look at it from my point of view Gise, I've grafted f'that lot – man an' boy – for twenty-seven, twenty-seven years. I'm clean, I'm smart, an' I'm brilliant at my job. Cor blimey! I clean streets, disinfect where dogs 'ave done their business, take old ladies to town on me barrow, polish the numbers on doors so the postman can read 'em clearly. 'Er Majesty 'as even sent me an award for efficiency –" here Malcolm took on a very noble expression; he looked like royalty in pyjamas.

"– Above and beyond the call of duty. And then I meet you and we get on brilliant – an' I think you're lovely you are. An' just when I think things can't get any better, what happens? That Willy 'I'm going to be the next chuffin' Mayor' Eckerslike bloke sacks all us street cleaners and gets this 'All-in-One-Der' monstrosity an' them rubbishy robots to do our work 'cos 'e don't 'ave to pay them any money. An' then to add insult to injury, I 'ear that you've run off with a perishin' lolli-pop-man. I mean, I ask you? I'm a skilled urban roadside and pavement specialist. He just leans on his pole all day, 'Stopping Children'." Then a thought crossed his mind. "Stopping children from doing what, I'd like to know. No, I'm sorry Gise darlin', I give up. You'll have to find somebody else – it's over…"

Rumble, rumble, rattle, clink! Rumble, rumble rattle, clink, clink, rattle! The tea trolley sounded, quite far away down the ward. This meant it was three o'clock when patients and their visitors were given tea or coffee and, sometimes, a jam sponge-cake left over from lunchtime.

"Oh no Malky mein chatz, you kannot be meanink that, ich liebe dich!"

"I love you too Gise but I've got no job, no perishin' money so this relationship is goin' nowhere…"

Rumble, rumble clink, rattle! Rumble, rumble, rattle, clink! That tea trolley was getting closer. It stopped next to Malcolm's bed.

"Tea! Coffee – would anybody like a slice of ca... *oooh arrgh oh gosh no!*" Just as the Voluntary Services lady stopped at Malcolm's bed, Gisele made one "last ditch" attempt to save the relationship and tried to put her arms round him. All this action – in the limited confines of Malcolm's bed space – was obscured even further by the clouds of steam coming from the tea and coffee urns. Disaster!

"No! I'm sorry Gise," Malcolm was announcing gravely, "when I say it's over, it's over..." And made a cutting gesture with his arm outstretched and a flat hand, as if to physically sever the bond. The sweeping gesture of his arm turned that gesture into a karate-chop which gathered momentum. And caught Gisele, full force, in the throat, just as she was bearing down to try to plant a kiss on Malcolm. Sending her staggering backwards into the Voluntary Services lady. Winding her and making her throw a scalding hot cup of tea – or was it coffee? – into the air. And we all know where that landed, don't we? Yup – *all* over Malcolm.

"*Oooh-Aahh-help!* I'm melting – Ouch – AAAH!" screamed Malcolm, his skin glowing red, then peeling away completely as the boiling liquid soaked into his pyjamas.

Within seconds that bed space became the next Armageddon. Malcolm was yelling out in pain, shock, surprise – or probably all three. The Voluntary Services was apologising and attempting to dry-off Malcolm's pyjamas with a tissue, which made him shriek even louder as paper-tissue is not the gentlest material to rub recently scalded skin with. And Gisele, herself in shock, was shouting at the top of her voice.

"Achtung! Achtung! *Nurse! Nurse!* Mein Malky ist dyink! He ist boilink alive in hot hospital beverages! You must help him before it ist too late und he ist scarred for life!"

"Quick! Get a trolley! Contact the burns unit. Madam – will you stop panicking, *please!*" The ward-sister arrived and tried to calm Gisele down but it was no good; her fears for her man were too strong.

"Kall der Fire Brigade! Kall der doctor, Kall anyvun! Kall no-vun! Kall somevun! You must help himm – ach nein, I am beginnink to panic!"

SLAP! WACK! SLAP! WACK! But the ward sister was good at her job. Expertly trained in emergency procedures, she spun Gisele round by the shoulders until they were face to face and gave her a hearty slap across both cheeks. Then did it again and again, until Gisele collapsed, unconscious into Malcolm's bedside chair.

Poor old Malcolm; his feelings for Gisele were so strong that in spite of his wounds, in spite of the sheer pain he was in, he wanted to calm her and called out to her while he was on the trolley being wheeled down to the burns unit. "It's alright Gise, darlin' – I've had much, *much* worse. Remember that time I was run over by that…"

But Malcolm was never to finish the sentence. As he lay on that trolley the powerful drugs that were injected into his bloodstream to deaden the pain kicked in, making him quite numb and he lapsed into unconsciousness.

Downstairs where it was cool, in the burns unit, Malcolm was treated for first, second, third and, possibly, fourth and fifth-degree burns and major scalding. The lady doctor who treated him, a Missus Pam Fry-Bacon wrote in her notes: 'If the beverage that Mr Tilsley came into contact with had been one or two degrees hotter he may have required plastic surgery.'

Hours later Malcolm was wheeled back up to his bed on the ward, where Gisele was dozing fitfully in his bedside chair. She woke with a start.

"Oh Malky mein chatz – ist you okay? I haff been worryink so much!" There was a little mountain of tissue-paper, shredded on Malcolm's bedside table; she had bitten all her fingernails down to nothing and was about start on her toenails. *UGH!* That's worry for you. "I am so ver' ver' sorry I haff given you so much pain. Can you ever forgive me leibe shon?"

"Don't worry about that, darlin'," Malcolm was chewing something over in his mind, "Listen, Gise, darlin' – that accident just now, that little dice with death has really made me think!"

"Nein, nein – Malky surely it vos not that bad…!"

"Let me finish, will ya! When I get out of here I'm goin' up to council, like. And I'm gonna find that perishin' Eckerslike bloke, like. And I'm gonna say to him… 'Ang on, what was I gonna say..? Oh yeah, I am gonna challenge 'im, them rubbishy robots and that 'All-in-One-Der' to a duel, winner take all!" Then the scientific part of his brain kicked in – remember how good he was at maths and science at school. "Hang on. That can't be a duel, can it? 'Cos there are more than two in the fight…" He thought for a minute… "Aw, never mind – we'll have a fight to the death. And there's gonna be one winner, me, know why? I'll tell ya why, cos I'm a human bein', I am. An' I'm cool an' I'm smart – suave even." He took a comb from the pocket of his pyjamas and ran it through his hair and even that seemed to inject power and enthusiasm in him – directly through his scalp.

"AAAH VUNDERBAH MALKY! Das zounds a little more like the man I haff come to know und luff. You must fight. Und I, Gisele, vill help you all der vay. Together ve vill make der mincemeat of der maniacal machines und exterminate der liddle fat dumkopf Herr Eckerslike!" No, she didn't like him either. Then, sounding a little more reasonable, "But first, Malky darlink, you must be getting vell again. Und all these blisters und abrasions must be healink. Gutte gott in Himmel, you are more red than der – der..." She snapped her middle and index finger repeatedly, looking at Malcolm quizzically.

Even from his sick bed, Malcolm tried to help her. "A lobster?" he suggested."Jawohl Das ist korrekt – der lobster!" She echoed, pleased to have arrived at the right word. Although we feel that really, Gisele knew this already, she simply wanted to get Malcolm to use those "little grey cells" a bit – her English wasn't that bad.

For another fortnight he remained at Suburbiaville General Hospital while his surface wounds healed, although it wasn't clear at the time whether the deeper wounds caused when the council repossessed his barrow ever would. Gisele became an almost permanent feature at his bedside. Every visiting time, in the daytime and at night, she would be there, talking to him, joking with him, reading to him, even arguing with him when he got depressed and crotchety – and that was on many occasions. Malcolm was not the best of patients. He would not eat hospital food, so every time she visited Gisele would bring a family-size yoghurt pot of her own concoction. Sauerkraut und banana milkshake which she would prepare herself at home before she visited. Adding to this mixture two raw eggs and a large Spanish onion, a couple of beetroot with salt and pepper to taste. Churning it into a yoghurty substance that resembled wallpaper-paste in her own blender which was, in fact, a butter-churn attached to a chain, driven by the pedals of her exercise-cycle. Oh yes, a very fit girl was Gisele, and thanks to her ability to pedal for hours on end, the "yoghurts" were kept smooth and Malcolm never did find out what was in them.

"YEEUUCK – what's in this!" grimaced Malcolm while Gisele stood over him one evening ensuring that he drank every drop, then handing him a spoon to scoop up the chunky bits with.

"It ist der secret Thunderhosen family recipe!" confessed Gisele, "it vill make you der schtronger man und it vill kombat those chemicals that are floatink around in your body. Now kommen sie bitte down der hatch. All of it!"

Malcolm did as he was told and drank and swallowed. As the days wore on he felt his strength returning, and he grew accustomed to the taste – although the mixture did not make his breath smell very nice – until the day dawned when it was time for him to leave the hospital. By now you might realise that Malcolm possessed the kind of personality that endeared people to him. Also, he had that open, honest sort of expression with a slight crinkle above the eyebrows that inspires trust in others. That afternoon when Gisele pushed him through reception in his wheelchair, there was not a dry eye among the doctors, nurses and therapists who had treated him. And rumour has it that even one or two of the doctors, who are renowned for their emotional detachment, are said to have shed the odd tear – including the lady doctor who had treated him for his burns, Mrs Pam Fry-Bacon who was so emotionally detached that most of the hospital staff thought she was a bit stone-faced.

As Gisele pushed Malcolm towards the open outer doors of reception the fresh air hit him full in the face, invading his nostrils and getting into his bloodstream, making it fizz and tingle. Those gathered were most surprised, Gisele too, when he raised a hand, calling her to a halt. She stopped, applied both brakes, to allow Malcolm to take those first faltering steps, then raised a hand to her mouth in astonishment as Malcolm broke into a run. Disbelievingly she gazed at Malcolm's form as it became smaller and smaller, eventually disappearing altogether round a corner. Then announced, "Ja! Das ist mein Malky!" And, once again, hitched up her skirt and galloped off in the direction of her man.

Chapter 9

The Challenge

Malcolm did not stop running until he reached the gates of the council depot. Then he remembered, *he was still wearing the striped pyjamas and dressing-gown issued to him by the hospital.* But it was too late to turn back and get changed. He did not have the energy to do so anyway. So he smoothed out the creases as best he could, tied his dressing-gown cord more tightly, and ran a comb through his hair. Habit ensured that he always carried a comb with him. It was as much a part of his immediate accoutrements as his pooperscooper. Although the council had repossessed that weeks ago and, now, held it under lock and key, secured by anti-theft devices in the town museum.

Taking a deep breath he pushed out his chest, shoulder-barged his way through the iron gates of the depot with a resounding *CLANG!* and marched towards the depot offices.

The usual crowd hung around, in groups of two or three, outside in the yard. People stood around chatting, finishing their "cuppa" outside in the mid-morning sunshine before starting work. This was a typical, everyday feature of the busy works-yard, the drone of idle chatter competing with other outdoor noise. But you could have cut that silence with a knife when Malcolm slowed to a walk; long deliberate strides, like a gunfighter of days gone by. His eyes fixed on Mister Bartholemew's office window. Even little birds became silent, the pigeons stopped coo-cooing and flying insects ceased buzzing. Then some joker whistled the introduction to that film, that western, *The Good, The Bad and The Ugly*. There was a quick ripple of laughter. It died almost as quickly as it began. This was serious. An ugly confrontation was about to take place, people realised. One look at Malcolm's expression told them that. That yearning ripple that creased his forehead had been replaced by a dark scowl, black as a thunder cloud. And the groups dispersed like townsfolk passing by in an old, television western.

The walls shook as Malcolm *CRASHED!* through the double-doors, the receptionist dropped the telephone she was talking into and picked up the internal phone to warn Mister Bartholemew that, "Some *looney* wearing striped pyjamas and a dressing-gown has pushed through reception and is making a bee-line for your office."

The internal phone was still ringing when Malcolm reached Mister Bartholemew's office. He never got around to picking it up. Without knocking, Malcolm pushed open the half-glass door to find his ex-boss knee-deep in a mountain of paper. Timesheets, job-sheets, workload distribution charts littered his desk and the floor. Plus there were one or two angry letters, from council tenants and private home owners complaining about the black-bags that were left in the street to be ripped apart by cats and dogs, as they were not being picked up until eleven o'clock in the morning and workers were having to run the gauntlet of "doggy-doos" and litter to get to work. The point all these letters were making was – this "All-in-One-Der" contraption was not doing its job properly.

Poor old flustered Mr Bartholemew was trying to calm these residents by typing a circular, a letter of apology to all those affected, using two fingers on a word-processor – he was not having much success and was on the verge of nervous exhaustion.

"Oh, Gisele, where are you for heaven's sake? You haven't been in for weeks – I've got all this work to do and then there's equipment to purchase, jobs to be allocated, wages to be docked, final-demand letters to typed, notices of eviction to be posted. Mister Eckerslike's shoes to be polished. *Slackers fired* – all work that I normally delegate to you!" Then he broke into a sweat. "Oh no – I'm running a temperature, I'm getting all warm and clammy, I'm having a hot-flush. *Now I'm breaking out into a rash!* Oh my gawd, must open a window. Give me an aspirin, someone. Anyone – *please*." Then he started to cry piteously, "Ur-hur-hur-hur!"

"Right Bartholemew – the worm has turned!" Malcolm announced his presence. Mr Bartholemew looked up, half angry at being interrupted, half in shock. Malcolm was the last person he expected to see, especially dressed ready for bed.

"There's gonna be a showdown," he went on, still out of breath, wheezing from his run from the hospital; well it is twenty minutes by bus, you know. "I challenge you, that Eckerslike bloke, that 'All-in-One-Der' gizmo an' them *ramshackle* robots to a contest. Man – that's me, Malcolm, versus that malevolent machine. And there is gonna be only one winner – me. 'Cos I'm a man and I've got a heart, then you'll have to give me my job back!" Adding almost conversationally, "Oh yes – there's more to me than a few wires and a handful of nuts 'n' bolts."

Suddenly the door flew open with a resounding *CRASH!* It hit the wall to which it was hinged. It was Gisele! She was out of breath from her sprint from the hospital in pursuit of Malcolm. She tried to catch up with him, had watched his rapidly disappearing form get smaller and smaller, until finally it vanished altogether when Malcolm turned a corner. "Malky mein chatz vhere haff you gone?" Her plea was answered. Once again, love lit the way. And this time that light led her all the way to Mister Bartholemew's office door – which, now, was beginning to sag on its hinges.

PUFF! "Malky lieb shon!" *PANT!* Gisele stood leaning, silhouetted in the mid-morning light, against what was left of the door frame. "I haff been tryink to be catching you up *PANT!* Ever since you left der krankenhaus *HUFF!* But vunce again *PUFF!* I am zhinkink I am losing you forever *HUFF-PUFF* – vhen you are turnink around the korner!" Boy oh boy was she out of breath; she gulped a great lung full. "But I should not haff worried because I followed our *love-light* und I am finding you here!"

At that moment Willy Eckerslike – alerted by the repeated door slamming and raised voices, some would call it yelling and shouting – in Mister Bartholemew's office came down from the floor above to investigate. "What's all this chuffin' screamin' an' shoutin'. By 'eck you'll 'ave them doors off their 'inges, I said. You'll brek 'em off t'wall, by 'eck!"

We have previously mentioned that Mister Bartholemew's office lacked a bit of space – there was barely enough room for Gisele and he to work. Malcolm's added presence made breathing slightly difficult. Now that Willy Eckerslike, who was slightly wider than he was tall, inserted his cannon-ball like body into those confines, the walls started to bulge – and a calendar, and a picture of Gordon Bartholemew's wife got knocked off the wall.

"Oh Mister Eckerslike, sir, god and infinitely more important person than myself. This is Malcolm Tilsley, one of your ex-street cleaners. He has come here – *HA! HA!* – in his pyjamas – *HO! HO!* – and challenged the council – *CACKLE* – and all its marvellous technology to a contest – *AHA! HA! HA!* - he wants his old job back!" Then he lowered his voice, "Naturally, sir, I've told him that the council can't afford to fund contests of this nature. A contest, I will add that he will only lose."

"Aye, y'reet there, Bartholemew, worra laff..." chortled Willy. "'Ere, 'ang on a bit, I said. 'Old y'chuffin' 'orses a mo..." A little burst of inspiration sprang to mind. Then it grew into an idea. So he attempted to place an arm around Mister Bartholemew's shoulders in order to speak to him in confidence. But because of his lack of height and the size of Mr Bartholemew's office this proved to be quite impossible, so they went into the corridor and Willy stood on a chair.

"Reet, Bartholemew," whispered Willy into his ear, "we've already spent next year's budget on that fantastic idea I 'ad about gerrin' that 'All-in-One-der' an' them state-of-the-art Rubbish Robots, reet?"

Mister Bartholemew nodded, drying his ear with a handkerchief. Willy Eckerslike had managed to lubricate it as he confided. He carried on whispering. "...So what we'll do, I said what we'll do, is let our Malcolm chuffin' Tilsley 'ave 'is day o' glory – reet?" He waited for another nod. Mister Bartholemew nodded. Mister Eckerslike went on again, "Then when t'residents see fer 'emselves how much time and money *I am* prepared to spend makin' sure *my* residents get t'best machinery money can buy. Then they won't be so chuffin' quick t'complain next year, when I 'ave to double their ground rates and land taxes to pay for it all…" He waited for a nod from his nodding dog. Mister Bartholemew nodded again – and cringed.

"C'mon Bartholemew," Willy ordered, jumping down from the chair, "I said c'mon!" Then remembering he was a Managing Director, soon, he hoped, to be the mayor of Suburbiaville. He jumped back onto it and had his underling, Mister Bartholemew, help him down and led him back into the tiny office, once again making the walls bulge.

"I have consulted my *dogsbody*, Bartholemew 'ere, and we *both* think that it would be *only* reet an' proper to allow young Tilsley 'ere to challege t' 'All-in-One-Der' and my *wonderful* Rubbish Robots t'duel – don't we, Bartholemew?"

Mister Bartholemew nodded again. Willy went on again, doffing his imaginary three-cornered hat and adjusting his imaginary mayoral robe. "The winner will be awarded t'contract for permanent employment by t'council." Adding gleefully, "An' we both know y'don't stand a perishin' chance, I said. Yer 'aven't gorra hope in hell." Then a joyous reminder, there were tears of mirth in Willy's eyes: "Yer 'aven't even gorra perishin' barrow – *HA! HA! HAA!*"

"Ver' well Herr Eckerslike, der kontest vill take place," Gisele promised, determined. Then she added tenderly, "But first I need a little time to nurse mein

Malky back to health. He has been ver' ver' sick you know und in der kranken-haus!"

"Huh!" replied Willy with a shrug of the shoulders, "Tek as long as y'want, I said. Tek as long as y'want – shall we say t'second Bank 'oliday in August. Reet, it's a date then, I said t'date is set!"

Gisele nodded once to confirm. "Kommen sie Malky, mein chatz. Ve haff verk to be doing – Oh, Herr Eckerslike, vun more thing. *I QUIT!* Und here ist mein notice..." Raising a flat hand to each side of her head elephant-ears fash-ion, sticking a thumb in either ear and poking out her tongue She blew a long, drawn-out raspberry, turned on her heel, and marched through the sagging door.

"MALKOLM!" He froze as Gisele's sharp tone battered his ear-drums. *"AT DER DOUBLE – VE HAFF VERK TO BE DOINNGG!"* And she double-marched him back to his flat.

The things Malcolm did not know about Gisele! For example, before the Berlin wall crumbled in 1989, she was chief trainer, physiotherapist and cook for the *East Berliner Ladies' Amateur Shot-put Team* and had brought many train-ing techniques with her to the west. She applied those techniques to Malcolm's rehab program. For the first week fol-lowing that meeting she ran Malcolm ragged to, "Try und purge zhose nasty chemicals from der bloodstream." It was the same boring routine every day. Walk, jog, sprint. Walk, jog, sprint. Between his back-door and his shed there was no break in routine and it wasn't easy for Malcolm to keep his mind on the job in hand. Gisele had him singing, laughing at the jokes she told him and reciting times-tables to relieve the boredom and take his mind off the pain he was going through.

Using her knowledge of cooking and skill with a liquidiser, she would make Malcolm up countless numbers of rich-in-protein milkshakes. Indeed some of these shakes were so nutritious, packed with vitamins, proteins and anything else that stood a chance in hell of doing you good, that there was no room left to put the milk in. They had the effect of making Malcolm want to use the loo a lot, a desired effect; desired by Gisele but unwanted by Malcolm, who was running out of toilet paper.

Then one day Gisele turned up at Malcolm's flat and gently told him, "Malky leibling – I zink you can be taking ze mornink off tomorrow und haff der lie-in – your rehab ist over."

"Sounds good to me, Gise, I was getting sick o' running round that back-yard..."

"Gutte – so zhen you will not mind if you komme to mein liddle cottage und

you vill go for der gentle afternoon schtroll in der park..."

****

"Malky darlink, das vos not you I saw
getting off der autobus just now, vos it?"
Gisele sat astride her bicycle, a large shopping basket mounted on the handlebars
covered with a couple of towels conceal-
ing its contents. She had on a pink track-
suit and her *"Team – Berliner"* running
vest, which had seen a few years' service;
it was a bit faded, there were dainty little
stitches here and there. Around her neck
there hung, on a leather cord, a referee's
whistle.

"Well," Malcolm answered, sounding a bit what-have-I-done-now? "You
said take morning off. *You* said we were
going for a stroll in the park. So I caught
the lunchtime bus."

"Nein, nein, nein, leibling I said you
were goink for der schtroll. I am ridink
on der fahrrad – now kommen sie. Move
das behind..." And with a second-hand
sergeant-major's swagger-stick (the previous inhabitants of her cottage had been
military people: a former Coldstream
Guards drill sergeant and his wife) that
was clipped to the crossbar of her bike,
she prodded and poked Malcolm around
the pony tracks in the park. After that
first afternoon when he hopped off the

bus, Gisele decided that was not going to happen again – and Malcolm did not know what hit him.

Using her knowledge of circuit training, a skill she thought would never be needed once she had defected from the East and the referee's whistle, she put Malcolm through the most rigorous training imaginable. She wanted her man back to his former self. And while she had breath in her body he was going to get there, whether he liked it or not.

Every day for a fortnight Malcolm would run, sprint, jog, sometimes forwards, sometimes backwards using Gisele's eyes to see ahead, around pony tracks, nature trails, the athletics track. And Suburbiaville Newtown has a very large park indeed. Every couple of hundred metres she would blow, *PHEEP!* on the whistle, and have Malcolm do press-ups, sit-ups, pull-ups if there was an over-hanging branch nearby day in, day out for nearly eight hours a day. She would keep Malcolm's energy levels topped-up with regular doses of sauer-kraut-und-banana milkshake, which she would concoct at home using her liqui-diser.

People love a *trier*, they like to see somebody making an effort. Early morning park users, joggers, runners and the like. Folk out for a stroll and horse-riders. Cyclists, birdwatchers and parties of school children out for a nature ramble. The tots from the local infants' school and others who just used the park because it was a nice place to be would look out for Malcolm and spur him on with cries of encouragement.

"Come on mate – you're doing well!" an early morning jogger would yell. "Go on son, push it out!" These shouts of support were helpful enough but the thing that helped most was when the children of local junior school recognised who he was. The whole third form of Suburbia-ville Elementary School were holding their summer athletics day in the park, when Malcolm ran past, prodded on by Gisele and the swagger-stick, urged on by shrill blasts on that darned whistle. They presented quite a spectacle to the hurdle-jumping, long and high-jumping, shot-putting, track-running and javelin-throwing kids.

Then one of them called out, "Look – there's Malcolm. *Remember Malcolm?* Best street cleaner there ever was, my Dad says!" and he waved. "Whatcha, Malcolm!"

Other people began to recognise him too and the word went out: "Malcolm is on his way back!" and he began to feel that he was not alone. Cries of, "Come on, son, you can do it!" would push him along when his energy levels flagged. "Go, Malcolm, go!" the children would cry.

That was just what Malcolm needed. He needed to feel that people were behind him, that there was a point to this training. Challenging the council to a "winner take all" contest was one thing but he realised it had been sheer bravado. That "All-in-One-Der", with that roller in front going round and round, those "Rubbish Robots" purging driveways and scrubbing the pavements and gutters. It was so fast – too fast. And he did not even have a barrow. But that child's voice made him forget those problems, it ignited a spark inside him. His legs developed pistons and he ran flat-out to the war memorial, an obelisk mounted on six stone steps just outside the park, climbed every step and like the hero of a film about boxing he had once watched, he jumped up and down with his fists raised above his head: the "winner", if only eh?

Gisele, on her bike, had to pedal quite quickly to catch up with him but she was very, very pleased now that Malcolm had suddenly been energised. She now felt she could begin *phase two* of Malcolm's training programme.

****

As luck would have it, that obelisk outside the park was outside the local swimming baths too. Gisele chained up her bike and they went inside.

"Come-on, *Gise,* you know I ain't no swimmer. Remember that day at the kiddies' paddling pool? I nearly drowned in three feet of water. That attendant had to give me *mouth-to-mouth resuscitation.* I've never been able to swim..." Malcolm protested to Gisele where they stood, shoulder-to-shoulder on the side of the pool.

"Zen it is about time you ist learnink!" Gisele's deep voice echoed around the baths and with a sideways flick of her hips sent Malcolm flying, with arms outstretched, *KERSPLASH!* into the water. Malcolm was still wearing his running shorts, his vest and the army boots that Gisele made him train in. It was a perfect swallow-dive, the only problem being that swallows are not very good swimmers and neither was Malcolm. The senior life-guard came running over to the poolside, and was about to dive in and save this drowning man. But Gisele warned him off with a scowl and a shake of the head. He was not going to argue with her, not with that fierce expression. Plus, with the weight of all those swimming medallions around his neck, he wasn't that confident he would be of much help.

Every time Malcolm grasped the side of the pool to try and pull himself onto dry land Gisele would tread on his fingers, and he would have to flounder about trying to snatch a breath. Luckily, that section of the pool was only two metres deep, so he could push up from the bottom and catch a lungful of the fresh stuff before descending to the bottom again.

In the end Malcolm tired of this and decided to try and make it over to the side. The life-guard was only too happy to give advice from poolside.

"Come on sir, you're doing well – cup those hands, pull the water towards you. Breathing through the nose, *pull* that water towards you, good! Kick those legs – that's it, you're doing well." Other pool users helped too by shouting encouragement, willing him forward. Wanting him to succeed. Oh, how people love a trier…

"Hey, I recognise you!" exclaimed the life-guard, "from the paddling pool." It turned out that this life-guard and Malcolm's savior at the paddling pool that day were one and the same person. They met and shook hands on the other side of the pool. From that day Malcolm became a regular user of Suburbiaville swimming pool which pleased Gisele no end. For Gisele had other important work to do involving her liquidiser and a sewing machine.

Late afternoon before the big day they were sitting on the wall outside Malcolm's flat when he confessed, "Look Gise, I just can't do it!"

"Nonsense, chatzy, look at you. You ist no longer mein liddle Malky, you ist mein gross stark herren. Do you zink ve haff been doink zis for nothink. Look at yourself – you ist haffing der butter-flies. Das ist all!" She was right. Since she had been training him much of the old the old Malcolm had returned. A small miracle had taken place, muscle had returned to his shoulders, largely thanks to the swimming. His legs felt like tireless hydraulic pistons and thanks to both Gisele's knowledge on training techniques, her liquidiser and the rich in protein milkshakes they produced, a lot, if not all of Malcolm's stamina, strength and hunkiness had returned. He felt stronger, fitter and more energised than he could ever remember feeling before.

Listen to this kids, habits like alcohol-ism, smoking, drug and solvent abuse are very easy habits to fall into but they are extremely difficult to give up, so it is better not to start them in the first place. Luckily, though, Malcolm possessed more than the average amount of will-power and with Gisele's encouragement and support, he was no longer feeling the need to go delving into dustbins, search-ing for discarded cans of hairspray and other dangerous substances that "should not be taken internally".

"Yeah but Gise, that Eckerslike bloke was right," Malcolm went on, "I 'aven't even got a barrow and even if I 'ad one, it wouldn't be my barrow, it wouldn't be 'Belinda', 'cos they've taken 'er off me. And I can't get it back 'cos it's under lock and key – and who knows what else – at that museum of antiquities…"

"Malky leibe shon, do not be worryink so. You must be conservink der strength und haffing much einschlafen." She shooed Malcolm into his flat, adding just as he closed his door, "Be leavink der worryink to me…" Jumping on her bike she rode flat out for home; an idea had been brewing for weeks. Now was the time to put her idea into action…

Chapter 10
Night-Time Break-In

Tewitt-tewoo – Tewitt- tewoo! Somewhere in the night an owl hooted. Crickets sang non-stop; *seesee-seesee*. It had been a pretty stiff climb of – ooh, maybe a hundred feet or so – onto the roof of *Suburbiaville Museum of Antiquities.* The walls were sheer, obviously an anti-burglary precaution, without handholds so the infiltrator had to climb a section of their own washing line to reach the skylight. A faint and constant scoring-sound of a diamond cutting through glass, followed by a gentle *thud* as the heel of a hand pushed a circle of the glass through.

Brief seconds seemed to take ages to pass before the cut-out glass disc, just wide enough to allow the infiltrator's body to pass through, *CRASHED* to the floor of the building shattering with an echoing *TINKLE*. Somebody must have heard that, security or a cleaner working overtime But lady-luck held, nobody came. All staff had gone home hours ago; the infiltrator had timed it to perfection. The museum – and Willy Eckerslike had shares in that too – would rather rely on its electronic surveillance equipment than have to pay wages at the rate of time-and-a-half to a night-time security guard.

Satisfied that the building was empty the infiltrator, Gisele dressed in black with a balaclava pulled over her head, abseiled to the floor of the museum. The hold-all belted to her waist by a belt through the handle made her body, silhouetted by the single shaft of moonlight through the skylight, appear a bit lopsided, like a camel with a puncture in one hump. Something else she had not mentioned to Malcolm was that before she had fled to "der vest", with the Stasi – the East German secret police – hot on her heels, as well as being chief-trainer, physiotherapist and cook for the *East Berliner Ladies' Amateur Shot-put Team* she had, also, been...

A *cat-burglar*. Well, the average weekly wage of an amateur ladies' shot-put trainer in East Berlin, even a *chief* one is pretty poor – so she had to make up her income somehow.

Disaster struck – when, as she descended to the museum floor she found she had slightly underestimated the length of clothes-line she needed and was left dangling about six feet above the floor; plus the pulley-system she had devised, by tying a number of sliding-knots in the line, snagged up. Gisele cursed the inferior equipment. If there had been enough time she would have contacted her grandfather, in Liechtenstein, a former mountaineering instructor and he would have mailed her the appropriate gear – but time was a thing she had little of.

This left her with no other option but to cut through the rope on which she dangled, then freefall through the remaining six feet, to land with a *WHUMMP*! on her backside – it was quite a jolt on the old coccyx you know, it made her eyes water.

"ACH MEIN BUM!" Gisele exclaimed, hitting the floor at speed. In a split-second she was up, rubbing her sore behind whilst at the same time scanning the exhibits thoroughly with careful eyes – the way she had learned years ago. Minutely surveying the museum displays, ghostly reminders of days gone by. They looked spooky in the dark; there were portraits and bronze busts of the architects, engineers and designers responsible for Suburbiaville's futuristic layout, a seven foot marble statue of Alderman Archie Tuck who had laid the town's first foundation stone – well, he was a big bloke. Plus other exhibits featured things like the bus-shelter with a self-opening roof, for use in heat waves or on sunny days. Also, there were the original sliding-doors from the indoor shopping centre. A revolution in their day; they opened vertically rather than sliding from left to right, and were designed in such a way that they could be dropped within two seconds, like a portcullis, on top of "smash-and-grab" burglars and ram-raiders. Unfortunately they had the habit of dropping down on innocent shoppers who passed beneath them, unaware of their function until it was too late. Eventually they were outlawed by health and safety experts when the casualty department at Suburbiaville General began to complain of an overcrowded waiting room. In the end they were taken down and displayed in the museum as a "novel but nevertheless unsuccessful" idea.

There it was. Located dead in the centre of the museum, next to a supporting column rising from floor to ceiling, was Malcolm's unwieldy barrow, "Belinda". Leaning against the side of the galvanised steel dustbins were his brooms and his pooperscooper complete with the snap-and-seal device, Malcolm's very own invention, still fitted. A cleverly worded inventory, or list on the post next to this display, noted this as standard council-issue equipment. It made Gisele extremely angry to think that Malcolm's ideas and ingenuity had been "poached" by Suburbiaville council to present the image of a council that cared so much, it was prepared to supply expensive equipment like this, so that the street cleaner could perform his duties "disease free".

Even Malcolm's bright yellow rubber-gloves were there, one was shown slung willy-nilly across a dustbin lid, the other had been strategically dropped on the floor, giving the impression he had just tossed them aside and had gone inside for a cup of tea. Gisele shook her head gravely; she could never remember Malcolm being so careless.

Putting on a pair of night vision spectacles, apparatus that she had cat-burgled from Stasi headquarters back in 1987, she took another careful look around. Laser technology sent beams of infra-red light over and around the entire display, encasing the equipment in an electronic spider's web of multiple beams. The web looked impenetrable; if one of these strands of light was broken it would set off an alarm at the police station, immediately dispatching the riot squad, a team armed with tear-gas grenades and pick-axe handles but no guns. Gisele *had* to locate the source of those beams. She took huge breaths, forcing her heartbeat down to a normal level. Until then it had been beating a passable rendition of the "Mission Impossible" theme-tune. In the past she often had problems with her adrenalin levels but experience had taught her to cope with these by deep breathing.

There it was – a single beam of light generated by a box that looked something akin to an oversized video camera, was reflected from mirrors, to others concealed in other walls and columns which created the invisible web.

With silent footsteps she made her way over to the box, stroking an imaginary beard. "Ah!" She had an idea and delved into the hold-all, rummaging around until she found a small, oblong pack. "Kaugummi – I knew it vos in here somevhere!" She took all six sticks of gum out of the pack and unwrapped them, taking care to put the wrappers back in the bag. If anyone did catch her, she did not relish the idea of being charged with dropping litter as well as burglary. Placing the sticks one by one into her mouth she chewed and chewed for all she was worth, until her jaws ached. Then *FLOB* she spat the minty wad into her hand and *SLAP* applied it to lens of the box.

Hey presto! The infra-red web was

there no longer. Thank the Lord for night vision equipment, eh? Gisele grabbed the handles of the barrow and made for the fire doors at the far end of the building. It did not budge; the rims of the wheels were secured to the floor by metal strips that were held in place by metal bolts. She selected a small adjustable spanner from her hold-all, and with bated breath she set about removing the bolts – at any moment the saliva in that chewing-gum could dry-out, rendering it stiff and unsticky, meaning it would drop from the lens of that light-projecting box and reactivate the alarm system. *While Gisele was bending down loosening the bolts!* She had to work fast.

She did, and the chewing gum held. Soon she had the barrow free and was making a headlong dash for the fire escape at the far end. Thanking the Lord again that the fire escape was not locked Gisele, Malcolm's barrow, his brooms, the pooperscooper and his rubber-gloves burst out of the museum and into the cool night air. The town clock was striking midnight.

With the *man in the moon* laughing behind her back, Gisele sped toward Malcolm's flat pushing his unwieldy barrow before her. She stopped en-route outside the local primary school, factories, anywhere that stored rubbish outside the premises overnight and putting it in the barrow.

****

Rat-a-tat, brrinng-brrinng – thump-thump. Brinng-brinng, thump-thump, rat-a-tat. Malcolm awoke to a deafening racket at his front-door. Some joker was doing their best to make sure he would be too tired to do his best tomorrow. He had been having this awful nightmare in which the "All-in-One-Der" had simply driven over him, crushing him and his unwieldy barrow into a mixture of flesh, bones, galvanised-steel and rubber. That machine was so fast. And those rubbish-guzzling garbage-cans had made such short work of clearing the remains that there was not even a stain on the pavement to remind the town of Malcolm's war with the machine. He glanced at his alarm-clock radio – but because he was receiving no pay from the council, he could not pay his electric-bill so it didn't work anyway.

He switched on his torch and stumbled towards the noise, wrenched his front-door open and was about to give the cause of this racket a good telling-off. "'Ere, give it a perishin' rest will yer. I've got to be up early enough as it is. An' I've got to try an' beat that blinkin' machine – with that roller in front goin' round an' round..."

It was Gisele and she was excited. "MALKY! MALKY! ANSEHEN *LOOK* – SCHNELL! SCHNELL! SEE VAS ICH HAFF FOR YOU IN DER BACKYARD!"

"AW – LEAVE IT OUT, GISE. YOU KNOW I'VE GOT TO BE FRESH FER THE MORNIN'." It had been a horrible dream, with really vivid images. "I'VE GOT TO GET SOME KIP! IF THAT MACHINE IS GOIN' TO SWEEP ME ASIDE – I'M GONNA GO DOWN FIGHT..." Then he stopped dead.

There outside his own front door was his unwieldy barrow, well, it looked like his barrow. "Let's see, now... Yup – it's Belinda alright, there's that dent in the front bin where the school bus run me over..."

Malcolm was beside himself with joy, so he walked round, stood beside Gisele and was about to hug her. But there was no time for pleasantries. "KOMMEN SIE MALKY VE HAFF VER' VER' LITTLE TIME UND VE MUST BE PRAKTIS-ING VER' VER' MUCH! *DER KONTEST IS IN NOT A VERY LONG TIME!*"

Gisele led him, still in his pyjamas, into his backyard. It looked like a tip – excuse the pun. She had emptied the contents of the galvanised bins all over his backyard and taken care to tread discarded ciga-rette-ends, old tea-bags, chewing-gum, sticky paper and whatever else you care to think of, and can be thrown away, all over Malcolm's backyard, before she had practically hammered his door down. The only thing missing in this slick was doggy-doo and Malcolm needed to practise the old *slide and scoop* technique that had saved so many pairs of shoes, to regain his manual dexterity.

By three-thirty that morning Gisele allowed Malcolm to flop exhausted onto his bed; his index fingers were still twitching, as though he was still squeezing the trigger-levers on the helping-hand and pooperscooper in an unconscious rhythm.

Satisfied that Malcolm had done his best she left him "out-for-the count" on his bed, his index fingers and thumbs twitching with an energy of their own, and went home. She had to walk too. She could not hope to control a bicycle, break into a museum and push that unwieldy barrow back to Malcolm's flat on the same evening, so for safety's sake, to guarantee success of the mission, she had left the bike at her cottage that evening. Blowing a fond kiss at Malcolm's door Gisele put her best foot forward. She would not be getting much sleep tonight...

Chapter 11

The Problem with Fizzy Drinks on Hot Days

It had been an unpleasant night, hot and sticky – typical August weather, Malcolm awoke feeling more tired than he had been when he went to bed. He could not sleep. So he had just lain there flat on his back, staring at the ceiling until finally fatigue made his eyelids too heavy and when they did eventually close that nightmare kicked in. You know, that one where the "All-in-One-Der" simply drove over him, mangling his body and his beautiful, although unwieldy, barrow into a horrible mixture of flesh, bones, galvanised steel and rubber. Leaving an unsightly, sticky *slick* on Willowy Lane, to be cleared, scrubbed and purged by those rubbish noshing robots. And all the time, in the back of his mind that roller on the front of the "All-in-One-Der" was going round and round faster and faster. *That "All-in-One-Der" was so fast.*

I'm on a hiding to nowhere here, he thought, but if I'm going to go down I'm going to go down fighting, I'm gonna show them nasty, perishin' nano-bots what it is to be human..!

KNOCK! KNOCK! BRINNG! BRINNG! THUMP! THUMP! – but very quietly – it was early morning, you know. *"SCHNELL SCHNELL! AUFSTEHEN! MALKY! MALKY! LIEBE SHON YOU MUST BE GETTINK UP!" BRINNG! BRINNG! THUMP! THUMP! KNOCK! KNOCK! "ZHERE IST NOT MUCH TIME!"*

Yes, it was Gisele – yet again. "Kommen sie Malky darlink get in der shauer. I vont you shaved, washed und shining like ein pfennig coin und be vasteing no time about it. Und zen hereinkommen der livvink room und see vas I haff for you!" Using the swagger-stick, she pushed and prodded Malcolm into the shower...

✳✳✳✳✳✳✳✳✳✳✳✳✳✳✳✳✳✳✳✳✳✳✳✳✳✳✳✳✳

The pavements, driveways, gutters and road of Willowy Lane were awash with debris. Thanks to an email sent by Willy

Eckerslike at the beginning of the month, well he never actually sent the email – he felt computer work was beneath him, so he simply wrote a *directive* and sent it downstairs to be typed up by one of the secretaries – there had been no rubbish collection for nearly four weeks. The recycling lorry had not collected any paper or plastic materials and empty bottles and boxes of rubbish, old newspapers, stale food, trays of eggs way past their sell-by date that had gone bad, broken crockery and stuff like that – were strewn across the ground.

Dustbins that had been filled to bursting were emptied all over the road, had then been re-filled again and had, yet again, been tipped all over the road. The residents of Willowy Lane were quite happy to contribute to such a worthwhile cause and were only too pleased to simply sling, fling or bung the contents of their ashtrays, waste-paper baskets and kitchen bins anywhere but an outside dustbin or rubbish receptacle.

The Willowy Lane Residents' Association went as far to organise special nighttime "burn-ups" in which anything disposable and flammable was burned and the ashes were just dumped in the road, to be kicked around and spread all over by can-kicking, yobbo teenagers and passers-by – obviously non-residents of Willowy Lane. A fashionable touch was added by chairwoman of the association, Spanish-born Seville orange tycoon and multi-millionairess Mrs. Ava DeCosta, when cheese and wine was served at these events. This meant that the Residents' Association was able to charge a fee to cover the cost of the wine and cheese, thus keeping away free-loading riff-raff and the events went down like "a house on fire", excuse the pun.

"Come and Party in the Poop", "Disco in the Dung", advertised fliers put out by a small but successful local printing firm; this contest was proving to be a "good little earner" and many small-time businesses were becoming a little bigger time because of it. "Come and Have a Great Time in North East London's Garden of Grot" invited a roadside café. "Welcome to bring your own sandwiches if you do not trust us". They raised the price of its beverages by £1.00 a cup irrespective of what the drink was. In fact, the only person not making "mega-bucks" out of the day was Malcolm. He just stood to get his old job back.

And to do that he had first to win the contest.

Dogs, attracted by general unkempt seediness of the area, did their business on road and pavement, on lawns, on driveways, even on a couple occasions on someone's front porch, but did people complain? No they did not. Rather than being repulsed by the revolting mess and smells, residents became quite proud of their ability to generate grime, grot and disease. Word soon got around to other posh areas in other towns and Willowy Lane became quite the area to be seen in, the height of fashion and if you caught an air-borne virus, you carried it around like a badge of honour.

News continued to spread. Many television and radio celebrities, some who didn't like to be seen in public unless they were wearing earphones, or they were behind a screen, began to visit Suburbiaville to visit "friends" because it was fashionable and a good career move to be seen there.

Each over-spilling dustbin, each discarded, half-eaten take-away, each canine misadventure attracted its own miasma of flies and the little hardware outlet next to Suburbiaville Central – remember that place which sold coolboxes? – also made a tidy profit selling army surplus gas masks and chemical warfare suits.

Willowy Lane had the look and smell, if you dared to remove the gas mask you had just bought, of a cross between a medieval fare and an alternative perfumery, a retail outlet that sold only the most offensive, disgusting fragrances permitted in a built-up area – we can be sure that if ever such a shop became popular or trendy, then a chain of them ranging across the country would soon exist – originating from Suburbiaville High Street.

Newspapers soon got hold of the story. A tabloid journalist from the Daily Reflector, a local reporter from the Suburbiaville Siren and a gossip-monger from that epitome of the gutter press, Views Of The Globe, were all there flashing their notebooks around, trying to get an angle on this scoop – and the more interest they could generate the better. So they spent their time weaving in and out of the crowds getting as many facts and figures as possible, then using a large dollop of "poetic licence", they would twist them round to suit what they thought their readers would like to hear.

The Artisan's Arms had set up a beer tent with a pig-roast, or the option of a nut-roast for vegetarians, on grass areas at either end of Willowy Lane. The aroma from both was irresistible and attracted people like a magnet, so Mrs. DeCosta felt it made good business sense to charge £5.00 a head for a single slice of pork, or nut roast. Proceeds to go to charity of course, however she did neglect to mention that the charity nominated was the Willowy Lane Residents' Association. No wonder she was voted business woman of the year. No wonder

Missus DeCosta had a residence on Willowy Lane.

The car-park of Suburbiaville British Rail station filled with purveyors of fast-food – don't laugh, some of it was quite edible and had only a few E-numbers. Mobile caterers arrived in vans, caravans, hot-dog vans and burger vans and a French bloke came on his bike and sold onions. All hell broke loose when a Chicken, Noodles and Satay van collided with Bert's Fish and Chips wagon while they competed for a pitch within the limited confines of the station car-park. Further confusion resulted when an air-borne division of the Women's Institute (WI) parachuted down from a hovering helicopter and set up a cake stand. Buns and rock cakes were thrown, insults were hurled, pages were torn from Women's Realm, the WI bible. Finally police were called in when knitting needles were brandished. The situation became very heated indeed when a wax effigy of Margaret Thatcher was set on fire and Suburbiaville's idyllic reputation suffered a severe pummeling when the whole thing developed into a brawl. Blood was shed when secretary of the group, Mrs. Elsie Crabtree, pricked her thumb on her own hat-pin. A peace keeping force form A-company, Suburbiaville Army Cadet Corps were eventually called in from its display tent to calm the situation. This was considered a useful training exercise by the commanding officer of the unit.

The Fire Brigade provided an engine with a turntable and extending ladder. No sooner had it arrived when it was descended upon by hordes of screaming and yelling kids; the air was thick with gruff firemen's voices, barking commands like, "OI – DON'T UNRAVEL THAT HOSE!" "GET DOWN OFF THAT LADDER!" or, "OKAY, SONNY – I THINK WE'VE HEARD ENOUGH O' THAT SIREN DON'T YOU?"

Children swarmed round the ambulance pretending they had broken their arm – just so they could wear a sling – or leg – because they *might* be given a walking stick. At one point the ambulance ran out of bandages. So that this did not happen again, the paramedic in charge, as there was such a demand, said: "Right – one cure suits all!" and lined the kids up outside his ambulance and treated them with a miracle cure which was, in fact, an aspirin stuck to the child's forehead with a sticking plaster. Some children went away feeling a little cheated, they felt they had been let down by the health service.

Bunting and streamers were draped, like gaily coloured spaghetti, from lamppost to lamppost. Large brightly coloured light bulbs flashed on and off between the telegraph poles. If you ignored the filth and that tangy sort of smell that reminded anyone foolish enough to breathe in deeply of open drains, Willowy Lane appeared very festive. This was not going to last forever and residents actively went out in their cars or in lorries to search for the filthiest, most obnoxious smelling refuse they could find and fetched it back to be spread liberally across the street.

Then the finishing touches were added: one was a raised platform from which future Mayor, the Honorable Mister Willy Eckerslike could doff his Mayoral hat, which he felt sure he would be presented with directly after the contest had been won, to the citizens of Suburbiaville. And the all-important start line. There was a finish too, at the end of Willowy Lane, but because nobody on the council really thought Malcolm stood any chance of finishing, not much attention was paid to that. No bright lights flashed there, no bunting was strung across the street, just one strip of ticker-tape was stretched between the big iron gateposts on the way in to the town park at the far-end of Willowy Lane.

****

Dressed in olive-drab overalls that added a slight military flavour to his appearance – they fit perfectly too, whilst allowing a full degree of movement, giving him the freedom to bend and stretch; we hinted at Gisele's skill with a sewing-machine before – Malcolm pushed "Belinda", his unwieldy barrow, before him, arriving at the start-line on Willowy Lane. Gisele brought up the rear on her bicycle, the basket on the handle-bars filled with bottles of muscle relaxing embrocation and arnica gel in case of sprains or tired muscles. Although she was confident of Malcolm's ability, if her past experience as chief trainer with the East Berliner Ladies' Amateur Shot-put Team had taught her anything, it had taught her to be prepared for every eventuality, so she was. Towels, bandages, aerosols, spare clothing and a flask of sauerkraut-und-banana milk-shake, mixed with a little prune juice – in case of blockage – made her bicycle look just as unwieldy as Malcolm's barrow. They must have looked a pretty weird couple arriving at the start-line.

Nobody could ever accuse Gisele of being a boastful girl but she could not help feeling just that little bit proud of the job she had done on Malcolm's overalls; the elbows and knees had been reinforced with day-glow yellow pads cut from his "Hi-Way Vest" and across the back of the garment, in fluorescent thread of the same colour read, simply

CLEAN, GREEN – *SUBURBIAVILLE'S FINEST.*

"An' 'ere he is," Willy Eckerslike's blunt, northern accent greeted their arrival. "All t'way from a somewhat less desirable part o' Suburbiaville. It's that paragon of 'ighway maintenance, Malcolm Tilsley. The chap who – *HA! HA!* – is gonna – *HA! HA! HA!* – singely 'andedly beat *my* 'All-in-One-Der' – *AHA! AHA! AHA! HA! HAA! AHEM!*" He went on as he often did. "An' in t'spirit o' goodwill the driver o' t' 'All-in-One-Der', Geordie 'ere, out of the goodness of 'is 'eart will give our Malcolm 'ere an' 'eadstart o' *five* 'ouses. Malcolm 'ere can even choose the side o't street 'e wants to clean. An' our Geordie 'ere will not even start t'engine until our Malcolm 'ere has finished cleaning in front of t'*fifth* 'ouse – worra lovely bloke. Ladies and gentlemen, I give you our very own, *Geordie the driver* - thankyou!" A ripple of applause sounded and Geordie raised his hands and nodded, then got into his cab, folded his arms across chest and pretended to yawn – giving an air of couldn't care less.

But as Malcolm drew up alongside that monster, Geordie somehow managed enough interest to say to Malcolm in an usually hushed Tyneside trill, "Alreet, Malky auld son – we both noo ye dinna stond a chance – so ah've gi'yer an 'eadstart o' five hooses. Then ah'm commin' tee' get yer…"

"You used to be my mate," Malcolm was about to say when a fanfare sounded over the tannoy system. DA-DA-DA-DA. *DA-DA-DAAAH!* "ALREET LADIES, GENTLEMEN AN' CHILDREN OF SUBURBIAVILLE. WI'OUT FURTHER ADO, AN' EVEN LESS 'ANGING ABOUT, LET'S GET THIS SHOW ON T'ROAD – ON YER MARKS, GET SET – *WAIT FER IT! I SAID. WAIT FER IT..! GOOOOH!"*

And Malcolm was off. Like a greyhound out of the traps. Choosing the even numbered side of the lane, he positively attacked the accumulated garbage on Willowy Lane, sweeping road, gutter and pavement with care and precision. Folding cardboard and paper and leaving it to one side to be picked up later by the recycling van. Doing the same with jars and bottles that were still in one piece. Pushing that wall of waste back with the hard-brush, farther and farther towards the slip-road onto the M25 motorway. Every so often, to add a touch of style to his performance, he paused briefly to run his trusty comb through his hair – very briefly, mind you. The thought of that big roller in front of the "All-in-One-Der" going round and round, faster and faster was enough to make Malcolm want to put as much distance as possible between himself and that junk scoffing juggernaut.

The hot August sun beat down, the miasmas of flies buzzed even louder, growing more and more irritated as Malcolm destroyed one pile of poo after another and rendered them homeless. He pirouetted; folding gracefully at the waist like an exotic dancer, he bent to treat stains left on the ground with a *SPLUDGE* from a disinfectant bottle. Gradually, but not slowly, he was making an impression on the mass of mess, and as he finished clearing the repulsive disease-ridden refuse from the front of the fourth house, he found he was actually *enjoying* the sport. Muscles in his legs, stomach and shoulders worked like pistons as he bent, stretched, then stood still, to empty a dustbin into his own galvanised bins, then darted forward to the next driveway. Before he knew it he had drawn level with the fifth house, so he dived into the driveway and attacked that.

"Kommen sie, Malky be der vinner, Who ist der mann? You ist der mann! Hip-ray, hip-ray – go Malky go! ZWEI, VIER, SECHS, ACHT WHO DO VE LUFF – KOMMEN SIE MALKY DO YOUR STUFF!" Out of nowhere – that basket on her handlebars was bottomless – Gisele produced a set of pom-poms and just like a cheerleader at the Superbowl she had been cheering him along every step of the way.

All the while Malcolm was reaping full benefit from Gisele's support. Rather than finding her singing a little strained and out of key – which, let's face it, it was; she could hardly have been accused of having a melodic voice – he found her harsh, Germanic tones a great source of comfort. The sound of support of the crowd, as well-meaning and positive as that was, might prove a bit distracting. Listening to Gisele's chanting, though, enabled him to blot out all other sounds and concentrate on the job in hand.

Back at the start line from inside the driver's cab, Geordie watched Malcolm progressing up Willowy Lane and found that he could not help being quite impressed at Malcolm's performance. Gradually, Malcolm was pushing that sea of sludge back and away. "But aw *f'cryin' oot loud mon* – ye've only just completed two hooses." And the silly beggar had stopped at the second house, because there was a brass number plate at the end of drive, to polish and buff it up. The hot August sun beat down. Ah've got ages yet mon, thought Geordie, pressing the button on the door – *ZZZZZEERWUP* the electric window opened. But, "PPH-WOOAAR CRIKEY MON!" When the stench from the build up of rubbish in the lane filtered in through the window of the cab, Geordie found it quite unbearable so, *PUWEERZZZZ* he wound it back up again until it was tight-shut and turned on the air-conditioning.

All this button pushing was proving a little too strenuous for Geordie, who was as it happens a big bloke – pretty fat too, probably because after a hard day's work, sitting in the driver's cab, he stayed too long in the Artisan's Arms – so he fished about in the "All-in-One-Der" glove compartment until he found what he was looking for, a can of fizzy orange. Opened it, *SSCHWPT* and took a long swallow. Pushed the driver's seat back to its fully reclined position, put the can of fizzy orange down on the all-important control box, his feet on the steering-wheel and cupping his hands behind his head, stretched out and had a nap.

Perhaps it was the aroma from the can that attracted that wasp; let's be honest, the scent of oranges must seem quite attractive to a wasp flying around on a hot day. But the fact remains, *somehow* a wasp got into that cab – probably when Geordie wound down the window fully – and hovered around quietly for a few seconds. Then, when Geordie put the can down on the control box, it flew down, got its proboscis out and had a good old sniff and slurp around the top of the can. By that time Geordie had closed the window, so when the wasp had drank its fill and tried to fly out again it found

itself trapped. It began to buzz around
looking for other avenues of escape,
there were none, so the poor, frustrated
wasp began to buzz louder and louder –
buzz- buzz-BUZZING around Geordie's
head.

"AW YE LITTLE BEGGAR GER-
ROUT MON!" exclaimed Geordie, and
swatted at the creature with a copy of
the Driver's Manual. He missed. This
must have *really* wound-up old waspy
because, buzzing angrily, it flew down
and *ZZAP!* stung him on the ear, then
ZAP! on the nose – that is how we know
it was a wasp rather than a bee – then,
for good measure, on the same ear again
– *ZAP! And you're out.*

"AW NAW MON – AARRGH!" This
caused Geordie great pain and he sat bolt
upright, kicking his can of fizzy orange
all over that *all important* control-box. In
a flash Geordie wiped most of the fizzy
orange from the control box with a bit of
rag, in spite of being in great pain. After
a further ten minutes' work had dried it
off completely, he felt quite satisfied that
no serious damage had been done and
was glad to notice that the upholstery
had not been stained.

But little drops of the bubbly liquid had
managed to seep *into* the control-box
which was full of intricate wiring, fuses,
anodes and cathodes and all the rest of
it. And oxidation stained all the shiny

metal surfaces a lovely shade of reddish-brown. Cathodes collapsed, resistors did not resist and diodes began to die but not all at once, although enough of the fruity liquid had seeped in to collect in a chain of little wet blobs along the lead to the AI chip, confusing the instructions received from the control box which, in turn, turned the clear, pre-programmed instructions stored in the box's command chip into garbled nonsense. Geordie the driver, was completely unaware of this – he thought he had cleaned it all up.

Some way up the street, Malcolm had just finished clearing in front of the fifth house and an invigilator, who had been stationed there, raised his arm to signal to Willy Eckerslike to start up the "All-in-One-Der".

"Alreet Geordie lad, power 'er up, I said power 'er up – let's get this show on t'road!"

"Phew! Just in time!" Geordie had just finished cleaning puddles of fizzy orange from other parts of the cab when he heard Willy's barked command. "Okay, Mister Eckerslike, like!" he called back and raised his thumbs, started the engine then ducking down again he flicked the master switch on the control box to the "on" position.

And all the time inside the control box, those little droplets of orange clung with grim determination to the intricate wiring to and from the AI chip, collecting in one large blob which dripped, SPLOT, SPLOT onto the circuit board and speed governor.

Then things started to go wrong. Like an army having received its orders, it deployed over the battleground. Some blobs progressed along wires to different components on the circuit board. Others using the citric acids they contained to eat into the AI chip's protective covering. The remainder branched off into the engine where they were turned into a gas when they smeared themselves over things like the cam-shaft housing and pistons. This would cause more damage when the gas seeped into places where liquid could not go – even more when the gas reached cooler parts of the engine and was turned into liquid again, clinging to those vital components. And you know that wire that feeds information to the AI chip is coated in a yellow polyurethane sheath, to protect it from contact with other components – well, the fizzy orange gas cooled down again to fizzy orange liquid again and came to rest on that and the acid in the fizzy orange began to eat into it. And then the thingamajig started to break up, the wotsit was soaked which meant that the artificial intelligence chip became quite unintelligent indeed.

Time, Malcolm knew, was of the essence but he could not help risking a glance over his shoulder at the "All-in-One-Der" and noticing a team of mechanics in overalls, looking over, under and around the beast. A shout rang out and white coated scientists rushed across to crowd round the machine, all nodding, scratching their heads and stroking imaginary beards, while giving sound, scientific advice to the mechanics which half of them did not understand.

"What t'perishin' 'eck is goin' on 'ere?" An excited, irritated Willy Eckerslike was hopping from foot to foot, firing members of the technical department on the spot and mopping sweat from his flabby face with a handkerchief. And the sun beat down making him even more blunt, bad tempered and downright insulting. Everyone else grew more and more fearful of his razor-sharp temper and his ability to fire workers on the spot. Jobs in Suburbiaville, these days, are hard to come by. Technical staff continued to swarm around the immobile machine, "Ah canna understond it mon!" Geordie sang but really he knew the cause of the problem – he was careful to wipe the evidence off the control box.

At the ninth house Malcolm heard an all too familiar voice order angrily, "Reet y'useless perishin' rabble. We'll ave t'go wi' just t' robots and nowt' else!" And that *yawning* sound of the cantilever doors opening. He did not dare hazard a backward glance. Perhaps he should have, for only one of those doors opened, releasing only two of the robots – who on finding that they were only two felt very lonely indeed. Rather than diving into driveways, shredding cardboard, breaking down boxes, slurping up liquids with their nifty little vacuum attachments and doing whatever else they were capable of, they bleeped and buzzed their way round to the other cantilever door – the one which was still closed – to bleep and buzz to the other two who were still trapped inside and so keep them company. "This is one of the problems with cyber-technology," explained the designer of the "All-in-One-Der". "Over time, if separated and forced to operate independently, the robots may get lonely." Apparently, later analysis revealed this had something to do with the robots' shared artificial intelligence and the fact that they shared a central plexus. Therefore they could not work as separate units.

By this time Malcolm was at the thirteenth house, he could not help feeling pretty pleased with himself and risked a glance over his shoulder. Whatever thoughts he'd had about being smeared all over the road by that roller on the front soon disappeared, for the "All-in-

One-Der" had not moved. Plus Gisele's constant support helped keep his thoughts occupied.

"We're a team you and me, girl!" Malcolm shouted to her, "and if I did win it would be thanks to you!"

But Gisele was not listening. "JA – KOMMEN SIE MALKY EIN – ZWEI – DREI – FOUR. WHO IST DER MANN WE KANNOT IGNORE – YA! IST MALKY!"

Back at the start line, the "All-in-One-Der" was all in. It was kaput but the one cantilever door was half-open – it would not open fully until the other door was operational – so with fingers crossed, Willy used his managerial directing authority to direct his staff unleash his final solution.

"REET!" he said, "RELEASE T'RE-MAININ' TWO RUBBISH ROBOTS!"

"But we can't, sir!" a technician answered.

"WHY THE PIGGIN 'ELL NOT. I SAID WHY THE PERISHIN' 'ECK NOT!"

"Because, sir," answered the boffin, "You just fired the driver and that's *his* job!"

"WELL REINSTATE 'IM THEN. I SAID GI'IM 'IS JOB BACK!"

Minutes later Geordie was re-employed to open the one remaining door, by hand-crank, and reunite the two imprisoned rubbish robots with the other two that were left inside. They were overjoyed and set off mobile arm in mobile arm, which was quite touching really. "AAH!" But they didn't sweep, vacuum and scrub pavement surfaces, they tore into front gardens and driveways ripping up shrubberies and scrubbed lawns until they were nothing more than bare patches of earth; that done, they attacked the privet hedges. In the end Willowy Lane looked like a building site. It was completely and utterly destroyed. They then turned on each other and started to *BASH!* into each other as though they were the remaining cars in a demolition derby. All but one robot smashed itself to smithereens on the other, using whatever attachment was on its arm to attack its partner. One, however, made it out onto the road and sped off down the lane in the direction of Malcolm and the finish line.

Malcolm – supported every step of the way by Gisele's non-stop cheerleading – was totally focused on the job in hand as always. With an air of professional smoothness in spite of the boiling heat, he guided his unwieldy barrow to the end of Willowy Lane. Neither he nor Gisele realised they had won.

Chapter 12

Willy's Promise

"MALKY! MALKY! You haff done it. *You ist der vinner – zis ist der ende. Yahoo!*"

"Crikey Gise – yer right!" He looked down the lane; the "All-in-One-Der" had not moved. It stood immobile by the start line surrounded by a mechanics and scientists in heated argument. He could not make out what was being said but many of the "technical" terms used would have made many a vicar blush. It was a bit like listening to a lesson in Anglo-Saxon for beginners.

"Oh well – if Mohammed won't come to the mountain..." Putting one arm round Gisele's shoulders and the other hand on "Belinda's" pushing handle he propelled them towards the start-line, feeling very proud of himself indeed – even prouder of Gisele and "Belinda", the two women in his life.

Malcolm had not traveled more than halfway back up the lane when, *BLEEP! BUZZ! BURP!* He came face-to-face with his arch enemy, or rather one of them – the other three had turned on each other way back down the lane. Having wrecked the front gardens and driveways of the first ten houses, having reduced lawns to bare earth, having reduced the herbaceous borders to scrublands, they found no more use for their mobile arms. *The Devil makes work for idle hands* – this being the case, they turned on, and began to dismantle, each other.

It takes a man like Malcolm to face up to one of these robot wheelie-bins with its red sensor flashing on-and-off, on-and-off, more and more quickly the angrier it gets. And these "Rubbish Robots" are not supposed to have any emotions; they are, supposedly, inanimate objects. Completely void of any feeling at all. Or they were until this whiz-kid technician, remember the bloke who invented the "dirt-dispenser"? Well *he* fitted an ego chip into this one droid to try and give it a sense of pride in its work that matched Malcolm's. This was the result. An angry wheelie-bin on caterpillar tracks with mobile arms, interchangeable attachments, a flashing red sensor and a bad attitude. And judging by the redness of its sensor – which was glowing brighter and redder with every bleep – this wheelie-bin's was getting worse by the second. Plus, in reality, even though the "All-in-One-Der" was only good for scrap metal, now, the control box was still intact. And still sending out complete instructions.

This poor wheelie-bin's AI chip just could not cope with the large block of instructions originally intended to be shared between four, from a control box that was operating as though nothing had happened at all. And it had, also, to try to somehow integrate this ego chip. Too much information – come on, you can guess what happened. It's not rocket science.

Gisele sensed something was wrong when the robot approached. Had she forgotten something? She twisted out of Malcolm's embrace and looked back down the lane – so that was it.

"MALKY! MALKY DARLINK! LOOK YOU HAFF NOT BROKEN DER TAPE AT DER FINISHINK LINE. IT IST STILL FLAPPINK ABOUT IN DER VIND AT DER EINGANG TO DER TOWN PARK!"

There, loosely strung across the entrance to the park, was the strip of ticker tape. The rules of the contest strictly pointed out that this tape must be broken by whoever arrived at the finish line first.

"SCHNELL! SCHNELL! IF YOU ARE NOT BREAKING DER TAPE DER KOUNCIL VILL NOT REINSTATE YOU!"

The robot bin did not understand spoken words. However it did understand the heat generated from Gisele's emotions. And it quickly converted this into bleeps and with the added input from the ego chip that ticker tape hanging loosely between the park gates was like a red rag to a bull, it simply had to finish the task. Like a bullet it sped towards the tape. Purposefully Malcolm, with gritted teeth, took off in the same direction. He just could not let this piece of tin win. This single thought helped him keep pace with the mechanical power of the Rubbish Robot, in spite of the sun, which was getting hotter and hotter as the day wore on.

Inevitably the bin, because of its mechanical energy, reached the ticker tape first but because it shared its artificial intelligence with three other bins, it could not work out what to do with the ticker tape. It did not know whether to sweep it, store it, suck it up with its nifty little suction device, shred it or whatever else robot wheelie-bins do with ticker tape. Therefore it just stood there, eyeing up this bit of ticker tape with its flashing red sensor and scratching its head – sorry – its lid with its mobile arm. This gave Malcolm enough time to slide in rugby tackle fashion with a pair of scissors and snip the tape – the winner.

And the crowd went wild. They went bananas. Some of them even went wild bananas. They rushed down the street towards Malcolm, surrounding him so that he was engulfed in a huge mob of well-wishing, cheering, congratulating and back-slapping residents – important people, some of them.

Lifted high on the shoulders of the crowd Malcolm was ferried back down the lane to the start line just as the town clock chimed ten o'clock; there, he was set down on the raised platform. Seconds later Willy Eckerslike emerged from the throng, prodding and pushing a rather harassed Mister Bartholemew ahead of him. Poor Gordon, the more he was bullied by his boss, the more stressed out he became and the thinner and weedier he looked. "Go on, Bartholemew," Willy threatened, "I said go on, gi'im 'is job back!"

Gordon and Willy climbed the steps to the platform and Gordon picked up the microphone. "Well, Malcolm – *ha* – you certainly proved us all wrong." Willy glowered at him. "Bartholemew!?!" Mister Bartholemew cringed.

"Er – um, sorry. I meant me, you proved *me* wrong. And we – er – at Suburbiaville

Council – um – er – think it only – ah – um – right and proper – oh I hate this – to offer you your old job back."

To which Malcolm answered, very politely indeed, "Well the thing is, Mister Bartholemew, sir. I've just been havin' a word with Missus DeCosta down the lane there – an' she 'as offered to pay me double whatever you pay me an' that's just for cleanin' one street. So thankee, Mister Bartholemew, sir. But no thankee, Mister Bartholemew, sir!"

And the crowd went even wilder, milling – as crowds often do – around the foot of the raised platform. One great, big cheering mass; but something was wrong. Where was Gisele? Malcolm caught a glimpse of her. She was just easing herself and Malcolm's unwieldy barrow out of the back of the crowd, about to go on to the cycle track. Almost beside himself with panic, he snatched up the microphone from the Public Address system and shouted, "We're a team, you an' me. I couldn't 'ave done this without you. Gisele, we belong together – will you marry me?"

A distant police siren growing gradually louder made it difficult for him to make out her answer. "Later, Malky liebe shon, but I haff to get this back before the museum opens at ten-zhirty. Zhey vill haff my D.N.A. you know."

****

And the newshounds settled, like flies. Attracted by the buzz, Malcolm was a hero and heroes create news. "There they are – it's Malcolm and that 'orrible little fat feller... Oh Malcolm – and I understand that this man sent hooligans to your home to steal your barrow!"

"Well I don't know, 'cos it was their barra in the first place, y'see. But it was in a rotten state when I got it, all dull an' battered – mind you that was a long time ago – so I painted it orange and add..."

"Foghorn Foggins, Suburbiaville Siren, Mister Tilsley is there any truth in the rumor that the council's Managing Director was going to double ground rate and charge an entrance fee to Willowy Lane later this year to pay for this 'All-in-One-Der'?"

"Well, I don't know y'see," Malcolm scratched his head then he noticed the loaded camera.

"No-one's ever called me 'mister' before..." He whipped his trusty comb out of his pocket, ran it through his hair and smiled and pulled his eyebrows closer together.

Isn't odd how the chance of a scoop can transform even the most languid of reporters into an Olympic runner? Well, here's a little snippet of information to back that observation up. Ace Gossip columnist, Hugh Nehd, News of the Globe, suspecting that behind the closed doors of the affluent Willowy Lane gossip was rife, lurked suspiciously in the crowd in the hope of uncovering any little gems worthy of creative journalism. When rumors of Mister Eckerslike's plan to double the rates and increase land taxes in Suburbiaville, reached his ears he made a bee-line for Willy, his notebook and pen at the ready.

"Hugh Nehd here, News of the Globe. Mister Eckerslike, *William* – mind if I call you William? Care to give us your side of the story – would you like to give us a quote; would you like to make something up?"

"No comment," answered Mister Eckerslike. "I said no comment. But don't think you've 'eard the last o' me, young Tilsley," promised Willy "nearly Lord Mayor of Suburbiaville" Eckerslike, from the foot of his raised platform, "Because one day in t'not too distant future, you'll rue, I said rue t'day y'crossed swords wi' William Eckerslike. An' tell that chuffin' driver he's fired, I said. Perishin' well sack 'im!"

THIS IS NOT THE END

Author's note: Since publication of this book, the area in Suburbiaville known as 'BADLANDS' has now become officially recognised by Ordnance Survey as 'MALCOLM`S WALLOW'

What a Load of Rubbish